Redeemer on the Roadside

(Park Bench Stories: Book 2)

by

Shari Broyer

Rights and Disclaimers

This novella is a work of fiction. Any references to real people, events, establishments, organizations, or locales are intended only to provide a sense of authenticity, and are used fictitiously. All other characters, and all incidents and dialogue, are drawn from the author's imagination and are not to be construed as real.

ISBN: **9798664231366**

Cover Photo by **Pete Linforth** from **Pixabay**

This novella is dedicated in memorium to

my brother, Carl Vernon Redden.

9-13-1959 ~ 3-23-2018

May this story bless your heart and fill it with forgiveness,

Shari Broyer

Table of Contents

Author's Note

Dear Reader,

We can always change our minds and be transformed.

This story of my brother, fictionalized, was, at first, difficult for me to write. I turned my back on Carl years ago, shut him firmly out of my heart, yet when I heard of his tragic death—he was struck by a car and survived a coma only to drink himself to death a few months later—a dam inside me broke open and I could no longer deny the love I still felt, deep down, for him. I grieved as I hadn't believed possible for the boy who had turned down the wrong road so young—who must have always felt lost.

So, I wanted to write a "what if" ending for Carl, what might have happened had he found redemption before it was too late? In creating this posthumous gift for my brother, *I* was made to see things differently, was able to forgive both my brother—and myself—and in doing so, rediscover the light of God (my own redemption) right where it has always been—within me.

May you also recognize (know again) Who dwells within you, and always remember, "There is nothing in this world that forgiveness cannot heal."

With love,
Shari Broyer

PS, I normally would have ended this story where you see the quotes at the end of The Road Home chapter. But, the small percentage of readers who gave me 3 stars or less for *Jesus on a Park Bench* often did so because they didn't understand my intention to create a short parable—like those Jesus often employed in his teachings—and they were disappointed that the story ended where it did. They wanted to know what happened next. This time, I also wanted to know what happened next, so I asked "J" to give me the Epilogue. I hope you enjoy it.

When you are finished reading, please consider reviewing this book on both Amazon and Goodreads. Thank you! I want you to know that I do read and appreciate every honest review. Reviews help us authors so very much in so many ways, not the least of which is improving our writing.

Also, those of you who have read *Jesus on a Park Bench* since I revamped the cover and made it part of the Park Bench Stories series may be wondering why *The Savior in Sunglasses* is not the second book of the series as previously announced in "Coming Soon" at the back of *Jesus on a Park Bench.*

I had written the beginning of *The Savior in Sunglasses,* but then I received the news of my brother's death a full year after it occurred.

It was laid on my heart to write this story, one I hadn't even planned, first. *The Savior in Sunglasses* is still a work in progress and will be released soon. That's why the first page of that story is still displayed in "Coming Soon" at the back of this book. It will be an actual sequel to this one because it is Will's story. (I was astonished to see how The Savior in Sunglasses slid right into place. "J" always knows what He is doing!)

Chapter One
Highway to Hell

He'd never been any good, not since the moment he had been born on Friday the 13th—an omen if there ever was one. His own mother had pushed him away from her, denied him her breast, shoved a bottle in his mouth and made his older sister, Ahyoka (nicknamed "Sissy") just four at the time, take care of him.

"Scrapper" should have been his first name because he always had the urge to fight. An imp inside would goad him to tease one of his four brothers until they cried or got mad and hit him. Then he had a good excuse to beat the tar out of them.

He argued with his sister when she tried to stop him, and he hit her back when she thumped him for not stopping. Once when they were older, he caught her right on her itty bitty breast. Man that was funny! At least for a few seconds. When he saw the look of pure anguish on her face, he stopped laughing. It must have hurt as bad as getting kicked in the privates if her expression was anything to go by. He had felt ashamed of himself then…but not for long.

"Liar" should have been his middle name because he could never seem to tell the truth. Another imp within would always conjure up a whopper to suit the occasion and slip it onto his tongue. Before he knew it, the prevarication came sliding out smooth as honey. That imp always smirked at how clever he was, and it got him in trouble sometimes. Ahyoka caught the smirk fairly often.

The worst instance was when their mother had made peanut butter fudge. Oh, how he loved fudge!

Mom said, "The candy will be set by morning. You kids can have some with breakfast if you'll wait until then."

He remembered how he'd lain awake all night, his mouth watering and his stomach growling with anticipation. Finally, just as the sun was starting to rise, he could stand it no longer. He snuck out of bed, tiptoed to the extra fridge in the laundry room and opened it, intending to sneak just one bite, but his third imp—the one who made him steal—egged him on until he ate the whole pan.

There were two other pans of peanut butter fudge on the shelf, so maybe his mother wouldn't notice if he moved them around to fill the bare spot. He hid the empty one under some bushes in the backyard and crept to bed.

Wouldn't you just know it? His mom discovered right off that the fudge was gone and started yelling, "Who took the pan of fudge from this fridge? Who ate the fudge?" She glared at all the kids, so he knew she thought they were all in on it together.

Sequoyah and Kanuna were still too little, but Ahyoka, Onacona and Wohali all said, "We didn't Mommy!" and the stealer imp told him not to admit he'd done it or his dad would whip him.

"I didn't, either, Mommy!" he said, and the liar imp smirked.

Sissy saw it and pointed. "Mommy, Waya's lying; he's got that twitch to his mouth like he thinks it's funny!"

"Did you eat the fudge, Waya?" his mom asked with a stern look on her face, hands on her hips.

He knew he'd really get it now for eating the fudge *and* for lying. His mom hated liars. That's how he knew she hated him, besides the fact that, whenever he tried to cuddle up to her and get some love, she always shoved him away and said, "Not now, Waya." It was never "now" for him.

"Did you eat the fudge, Waya?" she reiterated, the volume of her voice louder.

"No, Mommy, I swear I didn't," he answered, clamping his lips together tight so the liar imp couldn't smile.

Just then his daddy came out of the bedroom with his belt in his hand—when they were young, corporal punishment was still mostly overlooked—and Waya gulped.

"Which one of you kids ate that fudge?" his father demanded. "If you don't fess up right now, you're each going to get a lick around with my belt until somebody tells me who did it."

"I didn't, Daddy!" his siblings said in turn.

"I didn't, Daddy," Waya said. He thought somebody besides him would "fess", like Ahyoka, maybe, because she wouldn't want to see them all get a licking.

His daddy was angry; Waya could see it in the set of his jaw. He couldn't have said a word if his life depended on it.

"All right, line up!" Daddy barked.

Everybody started howling then, before they even got the belt. Sissy had to go first, then Onacona, then him. And golly, did it smart! After Wohali—who was younger than he was by about a year and a half—got a lick, his daddy was furious.

"Somebody had better tell me, RIGHT NOW, who ate that fudge!" his father bellowed.

"Waya did it, Daddy, I can tell," Sissy said, her eyes filled with tears as she glared at him like she would like to kill him. His mom was looking at him the same way.

"Waya, did you eat that fudge?" His daddy smacked the belt into his hand like he couldn't wait to give it to him, and a big lump rose in his throat.

The imp told him he'd better keep lying or he'd get it even worse. He swallowed the big lump and said, "No, Daddy, I didn't."

And even though they all got about ten more licks around and everybody was crying and rubbing their sore bottoms, Waya refused to own up to eating the fudge, not until Daddy, weary and spent, said, "Okay, I'll tell you what. Whoever ate the fudge, just admit it, please, and I won't whip any of you anymore."

That was what Waya had been waiting to hear, so he approached his dad apprehensively and said, "You promise you won't whip us anymore?"

"I promise."

"All right then, Daddy, I did it. I ate the fudge."

A big hand encircled his arm like a vice and spun him around. "Bend over, boy!" his father roared.

"But you said you weren't going to whip me anymore!"

"You know what, Waya? You lied and caused all these kids to get whippings they didn't deserve. Well, I lied, too!" Then his dad put him across his knees and whaled him with that belt about twenty more times.

Waya's bottom was so bruised and sore he could barely move for days afterward, and everybody hated him. So, at just five years old, he figured if everybody was gonna hate him, anyway, he might as well do whatever he wanted.

That decision set him firmly on the *Highway to Hell*, and he delightedly learned the lyrics to the song by AC/DC.

In his late teens, he picked up a guitar and easily learned to play the instrument by ear. Waya was a natural performer, at least that was what everyone told him—they all said they loved to hear him sing and strum, that he was so good he should perform in coffeehouses and bars. But he didn't want to work, not a lick.

It had been simpler—when he began to smoke, drink, do drugs, and often couldn't afford his habits—to steal the cigarettes, booze and drugs that made him such a hit with his streetwise pals. He'd already been shoplifting candy and toys from the store since he was a kid. As a teen, he graduated to slipping cigarettes and liquor under his coat, and from there he began breaking and entering homes around town, helping himself to other people's marijuana and cocaine stashes, stereos, TVs and even cars—if he could hotwire them.

He went to juvie then to jail, several times, but incarceration didn't stop him—quite the contrary. He kept right on, learning over time from his inmates how to "lift" things without getting caught.

His success in staying "under the radar" only fueled more self-centered actions. He could be charming and funny when he wanted to be, but it was usually only to con others out of something, or to throw them off guard so he could steal their stuff.

They all deserved whatever they got, to Waya's reckoning. They owed him. Everyone had been against him his entire life, since the day he was born. He was hurt, deep down, whenever he did try to love someone, because they never seemed to love him back, no matter how hard he tried. So, he covered up his pain with anger and lashed out at them, causing even further rejection. Thus, being unloved became a self-fulfilling prophecy, one he couldn't escape, because he wasn't willing to grow up and take responsibility for his actions.

Sissy, he knew, had tried her best, maybe even did love him, for he could recall some good times with her as they grew up—when she wasn't thumping him for being bad. She still tried to help him back then, even came to see him in jail, so he went to visit her a few times after he got out. Her son, Will, was in elementary school by then. Waya would stay until he wore out his welcome, mooch whatever he could off her, and leave.

He even brought his girlfriend and their baby daughter, Carina, with him once, and they'd stayed for months. The longest relationship he'd ever had was with Sue, mostly because she'd been able to make him feel loved by putting up with his selfishness and excusing his behavior so Ahyoka would keep giving him the benefit of the doubt, allowing them to keep staying there.

Ahyoka often got mad because Waya didn't do much to earn his keep, ever, but she usually forgave him—until the time he stole the money Will had earned by collecting the aluminum cans that littered the shore of Lake Erie.

Will had been saving for a new bike, and Ahyoka had planned to chip in on the purchase. When Will went to add more to his savings and found them gone, Ahyoka confronted Waya.

"You took Will's money, didn't you, Waya? That's how you paid for that six-pack of beer and that carton of cigarettes, isn't it?"

"No it isn't," Waya lied. "I got a job raking leaves for your next door neighbor."

Ahyoka opened the door and pointed to the adjacent yard. "Oh, is that why all those leaves are still covering Mrs. McEvoy's lawn?"

She shut the door again and continued her rant. "You've taken money out of my purse, more than once, but because of Sue and your sweet baby girl, I let it go. But this time, you took it from my son, and you've gone too far. Leave, Waya, and don't come back!"

Ahyoka stuck to her resolve that time, even though Waya knew she was heartbroken over the loss of connection with Sue and her infant niece. She wouldn't let them come back.

A month or so later—in response to a letter Sue had sent, informing her that she had broken up with Waya—Ahyoka sent her brother a card, wrote in it that she was sorry he'd lost his family, that she did love him, and she'd always be there for him if he ever decided to straighten up.

He'd called her, drunk, blubbering, and told her, "Nobody ever sent me a card like this before. I love you, Sis."

"I love you, too, Waya. I hope you have a change of heart before it's too late."

But the imps that had been with him since he was practically a baby had grown into outright demons over the years, and they weren't about to loosen their chokehold on him.

Waya found out several years later—by calling at a time he knew Ahyoka would be working—that Ayoka's son, who'd recently graduated high school, had been saving money to get his own place and now had a couple thousand in the bank. He wheedled and pleaded with Will to leave his home back east and come west.

"Take a vacation, man. You've been in school since you were three. Pre-school through high school. You graduated, and that's great, but you deserve a break.

Come on out to sunny Cal. You can stay with me until you get on your feet, and I'll show you the 'Waya'."

And Will, who was starved for male attention—his mother had broken up with Will's father before she'd discovered she was pregnant with him—lapped up the careless promises Waya set before him like a ravenous kitten at a bowl of milk.

Though no one, least of all Ahyoka, would ever believe it, Waya did love Will. He loved his nephew because Will always looked up to him and made him feel like he was somebody. Will was an innocent who believed Waya's lies, and that also made him feel good.

But because he knew Will was an "easy mark", Waya couldn't resist taking advantage of him the instant he stepped off the Greyhound in L.A. He suckered him out of some of his money right off the bat. "Let's go book a hotel room, and I'll get hold of a buddy of mine so we can score some weed and get high."

After that, it was only a couple of weeks until they'd blown through all the money Will had brought with him and were on the streets—which was nothing new to Waya, although it was to Will.

By then, he'd introduced Will to his drugs of choice, meth and heroin. He taught Will to lie and steal just as he did to avoid withdrawals, and they slummed their way along together.

Sissy had come to California several times to beg Will to stop doing drugs, promising to help him any way she could to get a good job and start over. But by then the hold Waya and the drugs had on Will was firmly cemented, and Will wouldn't, couldn't stop. He also didn't want to work any more than Waya did. Why pay rent when you could wheedle a place to stay for a night or two, go to a shelter, or build a "street house" to live in? Why slave away at some job when you could steal and panhandle your way through life?

Ahyoka really hated Waya for this. She stopped coming to California, changed her number, cut off all contact with her brother and her son.

And then Waya had the accident. He'd stolen a bike from another homeless "friend", told him he just wanted to borrow it for a couple of hours but didn't give it back.

Last thing Waya knew, he was riding along on the berm of the Pacific Coast Highway, for once not under the influence of any substance or even hungover, enjoying the view of the ocean and the balmy breeze that blew off it. Then a car slammed into the back of his bicycle, and he went hurtling through the air to crash land on his helmet-less head atop the rocky cliffs just beyond the guardrail.

A stranger who'd been driving in the opposite direction saw the whole thing, watched as the motorist hit the man on the bicycle with his fancy Porsche and didn't stop, just kept going without a backward glance.

The stranger turned his Toyota Camry around at the first turnoff and drove back to the scene of the accident, put on his emergency flashers, scrambled over the console and got out of the passenger side of the car. When he saw the man was bleeding profusely from his head, he knew time was of the essence, so he didn't bother calling an ambulance.

He climbed over the metal barrier onto the cliff to gently lift the unconscious, broken man into his arms and returned to his car where he laid him carefully on the backseat then drove to the nearest hospital.

Chapter Two
Awakenings

The hospital staff was in awe of the quiet, nice-looking guy who came daily to sit with the comatose man he didn't even know. Mr. Jay King had long caramel-colored hair, that was evident, but he wore it swept up neatly into a man bun, and though his clothes were casual—light-colored twill slacks and pastel-colored polo shirts—they were of good quality, as were his sneakers. They all thought Mr. King was a hero for bringing the unknown street person in for treatment and insisting that he be allowed to visit in lieu of family. Not many would do that today.

But every morning for the past two months, Jay King had arrived on the dot of nine to spend most of the day with the victim, ceaselessly talking to him in a kind, gentle voice, calling for assistance when John Doe started exhibiting withdrawal symptoms: restless legs, face contortions, diarrhea, cold sweats. (Dr. Wellington ordered morphine injections.)

On this particular Friday—which just happened to be September 13th and, unbeknownst to the others, the patient's 44th birthday—a young nursing student named Jen could no longer contain her curiosity. She crept over to the door of the room the John Doe had been moved to several weeks ago after he stabilized and no longer needed to be kept in ICU. She listened there for a few minutes and returned to tell the others, "All this time, Mr. King has been praying for that comatose patient! I heard him say, 'I know it is Your will, Father, so I ask You to bring this man out of his coma.' He just keeps repeating those same words over and over."

Mallory, the CNA on duty, said "Really?" and her eyebrows rose nearly to her hairline.

Sadie, the head RN, snorted and said, "I don't know why he's bothering. John Doe's gonna die, anyway, and if he doesn't, he's likely to have brain damage. That coma is persistent."

"Yeah," Jen said, "but Mr. King is persistent, too."

Sadie shook her head. "Wasting his time's more like it."

In that instant, the EEG and cerebral oximetry readers on John Doe's vitals monitor began beeping, indicating an event. Sadie, Jen and Mallory went rushing into his room. Mallory gasped—she couldn't help it—and Sadie instantly shot her a disapproving look. Emotional reactions were highly discouraged in the medical profession, and Mallory had received training regarding this fact.

What they saw before them was John Doe, awake and scowling, asking Mr. King in a weak, scratchy voice what he was doing there.

"Oh my heavens!" Jen cried, and Sadie sent her a quelling look, too.

Stepping forward, the RN said, "Sir, we don't know your name—"

"It's Waya Ridge," the patient interrupted.

Sadie continued as if he hadn't spoken. "—but you had an accident, and this man sitting beside your bed brought you in. I need to make some notations of what's on your monitor right now, and then we'll call Dr. Wellington to come and do a thorough check of you. How are you feeling?"

"Like my head's been cracked open," he told her.

Nearly finished jotting things down on his chart, like the time of the event, vital signs, and the patient's real name, Sadie added the words, "Pt. seems coherent." Then she responded to his remark, "That's because it has. You literally cracked your skull when you flew off your bicycle onto the rocky cliffs."

"Can I have some water?" Waya requested.

Sadie gestured for Mallory to pour him some using the glass provided in the admissions kit: plastic tub, plastic pitcher, plastic drinking glass, plastic emesis basin, body lotion and a box of tissues.

The CNA handed the glass to Sadie, and the RN held a straw to Mr. Ridge's lips to allow him a small sip, after which he immediately said, "Uh-oh, I think I'm gonna be sick."

"That's to be expected; you haven't had anything going down your esophagus for a while," Sadie informed him as she held the emesis basin to his mouth so he could vomit back up the small amount of water.

When Waya's nausea had passed and Sadie had wiped his mouth with a tissue, he croaked, "How did the accident happen?"

"Someone driving too close to the side of the road slammed into the back end of your bike on the Pacific Coast Highway," Jay King answered him. "I was headed the other way when I saw him hit you and keep going. I turned around as soon as I could, drove back, saw that you'd die without immediate medical attention, and brought you here."

Though Waya couldn't remember a thing about the day of the accident, he did recall how miserable he'd been in the days (and years) just prior, how it had felt to be a slave to the heroin and life on the streets long after these things ceased to be easy, free and fun.

Years ago, Waya had realized that the supposed "good times" were really just temptations the imps had dangled in front of him to keep him trotting after them like some dumb pony trapped in a never-ending wheel ride, but he couldn't stop. He'd thought about killing himself over and over again, especially when he couldn't get his fix and started having withdrawals, but he was too afraid to do it.

"Why didn't you just leave me on the roadside, like the useless piece of trash I am?" Waya spat.

Jay looked at him with gentle, topaz brown eyes and answered in a soothing tone, "It's not God's will that even one of His little ones should perish. You live because His grace transcends your desire for death. If you will allow it, that grace can give you a whole new life."

In that instant, Waya's eyelids fluttered closed, and he dreamed, following a quick succession of images of himself roaming free with his siblings as a child, exploring, climbing trees, running through open meadows, swimming in creeks and lying on the sun-warmed blacktop of seldom-used roads to dry. Building forts with Sissy and his brothers, nibbling on plants and berries to see if they were good before consuming them—spitting them out if they tasted bad—things like that had come naturally to him. That was what he was made for—living free. It was in the very marrow of his bones; in the primitive, type O blood that coursed through his veins, in his Native American, Cherokee heritage. "Want mustard flower stems," he muttered, his eyes rolling dazedly as he awoke, and the staff just thought he'd lost coherence because he'd been temporarily unconscious.

Waya didn't know if he wanted "a whole new life". He wanted the life he'd had when he and his siblings were young. He had never been able to adapt to the real world and had been living on the streets for 26 years, since the day he'd turned eighteen and his mother threw him out of the house.

A few times when the imps went into hiding for some reason unknown to him, he'd vow to go straight, but it felt too foreign; he got fired within a week or two each time he attempted to work a regular job—usually because he'd have to get a fix and so failed their drug tests—and after a while, no one would hire him, anyway.

"A whole new life, huh? I've tried that before. It never worked."

Mr. Ridge was agitated, Sadie could tell because his blood pressure was all over the place. "Mr. King, I'm sorry, but the patient is getting upset, so I'll have to ask you to leave now."

Jay nodded then rose from his chair and left the room without protest. Waya immediately succumbed to oblivion again.

Chapter Three
The Second Day

The next morning promptly at 9:00, Jay returned and went directly to Mr. Waya Ridge's room.

Waya, who was awake and watching television, glanced over as his visitor entered the room and scowled. "I don't want to watch this show, but I can't get to the remote all trussed up like this." He nodded his head in the direction of his hands, which were bound to the bedrails with restraints so he wouldn't dislodge his intravenous needles.

Jay looked up at the TV monitor and smiled. "Oh, but this was one of the best programs any man has ever produced!"

"Are you kidding me? Do you really think *Highway to Heaven* was the 'best'? Come on! It's too syrupy sweet, for one thing, and it's ancient for another. I couldn't believe it was still being aired anywhere, but there it is."

"Just watch it," Jay urged. "I think you might change your mind."

They watched the first half of the pilot episode, in which Jonathan Smith visited a rest home and made things better for the residents.

When the man in the truck told Jonathan he'd have to pay ten dollars for a ride to the home, Waya said, "That's right buddy, nothin' in this world is free." Then the man repeated that very sentiment and Waya laughed. "This is better than I thought," he said.

Jay picked up the remote and paused the show. "Waya, I happen to know that you got a whole lot from 'this world' for 'free'. Only it wasn't given to you; you took it."

Waya ignored Jay's words. "Un-pause it," he ordered.

Jay obeyed. At that instant Jonathan said, "Kindness is free," and Waya snorted, but he kept watching, almost in spite of himself.

He only reacted twice, once to turn his head away when Jonathan brought bicycles to his co-worker so that he and she could ride to work together instead of walking; and again to cheer when the co-worker's brother, an ex-cop, got into a fight in a bar and was beaten up. "Damned pigs!" he exclaimed.

"Waya, no one is 'damned'. Not even you," Jay said.

When the program was over, Waya remarked, "I sure don't want to watch the second half of this. It's all a bunch of hooey designed to keep 'good Christians' believing in a reward coming to them in the hereafter. There are no rewards, only hell on earth! AC/DC got it right with my favorite song, *Highway to Hell.*"

Jay shook his head. "It is true that there are no rewards in the 'hereafter', there is only NOW in Heaven; however, it's very sad that you have never learned that God is ALL WAYS and ALL ROADS. There are many trails that you may follow. But the easiest path is the one that leads you inward, for you are part of Him, and you will always find Him—and your rewards—there."

Waya scowled. "I don't believe in God. If God is always there, why did He let me grow up so unloved?"

"You were never unloved, beloved son of God."

"It sure felt like it!" Waya insisted. "My own mother hated me. My brothers and my sister still do."

"Your mother was a victim of her own wrong-mindedness. She was tired when she gave birth to you after three previous pregnancies, one of which was a stillborn boy, a brother you never knew. She was more than tired. She was deeply depressed and believed there was no way out of the situation her own willfulness had created. And she was still a very young woman, a child herself, really. Remember, she had your sister, her firstborn, at just seventeen."

Waya felt a twinge of sympathy for his mom at Jay's words, but he still felt great anger toward her, too, even though she was gone. He shook his head. "No matter what, a mother should love her own child!"

"Yes, she should, but your mother just wasn't able to. That was never your fault."

Tears sprang up in Waya's eyes, and he blinked them away furiously. "What about Sissy, and the boys, huh? What excuse did they have not to love me?" But even as he said the words, Waya knew that he himself had caused them to hate him. "Okay, okay," he said, forestalling any answer Jay might have voiced. "So I didn't always do right by them, but they didn't always do right by me, either. What about forgiveness, huh?"

"Waya," Jay said gently, "you were always forgiven, but you refused to accept it. You kept acting the part of the unforgiven, which rendered your siblings unable to hold onto any desire for reconciliation they might have had. And remember, they too, were incapable of feeling God's love. They struggled with their own demons due to the dysfunctional way you all grew up."

Heaving a great sigh, Waya turned his head away. "I'm not sure how you know all this Jay, but I don't care. Leave now. I've had enough of your lectures for one day." He lost consciousness again.

The women who had been taking care of him—Sadie, Jen and Mallory—started to wonder if Waya Ridge somehow awoke just for these visits from Mr. King.

Chapter Four

Two Months Earlier

(July & August)

Her cell phone rang, and Ahyoka picked it up to glance at the screen. The number wasn't one she recognized, but it had a California area code, so she answered rather than hitting Ignore like she usually did with unknown numbers. Hope that it might be her son flared within her.

"Hello, who is this, please?"

"Is this Ahyoka Ridge?" a man asked.

"Who *is* this?" Ahyoka insisted.

"My name is Jay King, and I'm calling about your brother."

Sighing with disappointment, she asked, "Which one?"

"Waya."

"Sorry, but whatever it is, whatever he's done, I don't care. I'm hanging up now."

"He's in a coma," Mr. King said quickly.

Despite her insistence that she didn't care about Waya, the mothering instinct she'd always had for her siblings stirred, and before she could stop the instantaneous reaction, she cried, "What?!"

"He's in a coma," the stranger repeated gently. "He was in an accident, hit and run, was left for dead on the side of the road, and now he's in a coma. He's a patient at Kindred Hospital in Los Angeles, if you would like to come and see him."

Resolutely, Ahyoka hardened the heart that had softened for an instant. "Thank you for telling me," she said, and hung up.

A week later, after Ahyoka had had several battles with herself regarding her comatose brother, the brother she had—in the Cherokee tradition—declared dead to her, her cell phone rang again. Because she hadn't blocked the number after Jay King had called, nor had she saved it, she didn't recognize the California number, and again she answered hoping it would be her son.

"Hello?"

"Ahyoka, this is Jay King calling again," the mild voice stated. "I just thought you might like to know that your brother is still in the coma."

"Look, Mr. King, I'm not my brother's keeper. Waya's been dead to me for the last six years. I haven't contacted him, and he sure hasn't bothered to contact me. Why should I care now if he's still in a coma, or whether he lives or dies?"

"I believe there is that within you that still loves him, regardless of anything he's done," Mr. King told her.

"I assure you, you're wrong," Ahyoka replied, again stifling the surge of concern that tried to rise to the forefront of her conscience. "Please don't call me again. I'm blocking this number as soon as I hang up." She hit End and did exactly that.

But then guilt plagued her as she recalled that her mother had asked her, on her deathbed, to "take care of" her brothers. Ahyoka had always done that, and she'd also taken care of her mother when Galilahi's body could no longer tolerate her excesses. Her mother had been a heavy smoker and an abuser of prescribed medications, especially Vicodin.

Even though she'd mumbled that she would keep the family together to ease her mother's passing, Ahyoka had no intention of doing so. It was her chance, at long last, to be free of the unfair burdens her mom had always heaped upon her.

She'd deliberately lied, deliberately broken the promise, deliberately turned her back on the rest of her siblings because every one of them had gotten into substance abuse, and she didn't want them anywhere near her. Prior to her mother's death, Ahyoka had barely tolerated them when they came around while she was caretaking her mom, but that grudging forbearance stopped when Galilahi died.

Ahyoka also didn't want anything more to do with her siblings because they always used her if she gave them a chance. And Waya had done worse than any of them; he'd not only used her, he'd used her son and led him into drug abuse, as well.

The only exceptions were Onacona and Wohali. They hadn't lived long enough to use her. Grief welled up anew as she thought of them now.

Onacona, her first "Bubba" had been found dead when he was on the threshold of young manhood in a bizarre unsolved mystery. He had been the one, though younger than she was by fifteen months, to comfort her when the nightmares came. Growing up, they gave each other solace through daily talks about their hopes and dreams of getting away and living a better life. She couldn't have gotten through their dysfunctional childhood without him.

When Onacona passed, Ahyoka had been inconsolable with grief. Wohali, just twelve years old, said, "Sissy, I'll be your Bubba now." And he had later been her comfort through the years of young, single motherhood—bringing her groceries, giving her cash, taking her out to enjoy life once in a while. He was the only one of the four brothers left who cared about what *she* needed.

Then Wohali, who had always had a strong addictive nature but fought it continually, succumbed to meth in order to stay awake the overlong hours necessary to get his new business—making and delivering specialty parts all over the country—off the ground. Methamphetamine was the death of him. He took his own life at the age of 28 to escape the hold the drug had over him.

Shaking off the pain that the addictions of her family had caused her since she was a girl, Ahyoka went on about her own life, telling herself that Waya had chosen his consequences, they were nothing to do with her.

A month later, another unknown California number displayed on her cell phone screen. This time, she quashed the hope that flared within her and answered in a flat voice, "Hello."

"Ahyoka, it's Jay King. I thought you might like to know that Waya is still in the coma."

Anger flared within her. "Why are you calling me again after I asked you not to?" she demanded.

"Because, I believe there is that within you that still loves Waya, regardless of anything he's done," Mr. King reiterated what he'd said the last time.

Ignoring the uncomfortable twinge his words caused her, Ahyoka said, "You've never even met me, Mr. King. How can you be so sure that I still care about my brother?"

"Ah, but I have met you. It was years ago, when you were a little girl, but you've forgotten. I remember, though. I carry a picture of you back then with me today. I know how passionately protective you were of Waya—and all your brothers."

"So you've got some picture of me in your pocket and you remember that I defended Waya sometimes when we were kids. What does that prove?"

"Once someone is in your heart, they are there forever. You can make them 'dead' to you, but you can never lose the love you once felt for them, no matter what you do, Ahyoka. Love is the only reality, and it is eternal."

Mr. King's words got to her, although Ahyoka wouldn't admit it to him—or to herself—at that moment. She jabbed the End button on her phone and blocked the number.

"Boy does that man ever think he knows it all," Ahyoka muttered under her breath inside her cubicle as she turned back to the work in front of her. Her day job as a data entry clerk for a worldwide online payments company was very demanding, as was her night job as a medical transcriptionist. For five days out of seven, Ahyoka pushed herself to inhuman limits. It was the only way she could keep the failures of having an addict son and her divorce from an alcoholic ex-husband from haunting her.

On weekends she was so exhausted, she slept in both days, arising to frantically clean her home and do weeding and yardwork as needed in the mornings then ready everything for the week to come in the afternoons: wash and iron clothes, cook meals for seven days and freeze them, pack Monday's lunch ahead of time, etc.

All this busy-ness also kept her from focusing too much on how isolated and alone she felt.

When she got home that night, however, Ahyoka was unable to block out the voice of Mr. King in her head. The reminder that she still loved her brother stuck like a burr as she nuked her pre-made supper of soup and made a small salad to go with it. The stranger's words clung tight as she poured herself a glass of wine—always and ever only one—to go along with dinner. Even while she watched her favorite 45 minute show via the Internet as she ate, what Mr. King had said persisted. No matter how hard she tried to ignore them, the words she didn't want to hear wouldn't stop replaying in her mind.

Her eyes filled with tears that she dabbed angrily. She wouldn't cry over Waya; she WOULD NOT. Finally, Ahyoka started her transcription work early to blot out the pain. She could always rely on her two jobs to accomplish that.

But, it turned out that Ahyoka couldn't count on her work to keep thoughts of Waya at bay. The image of him flying through the air and landing on his head haunted her dreams. Often, over the next three weeks, she awoke with tears on her cheeks.

At moments during her day job—such as when she grabbed a cup of coffee during her break—memories of her brother that made her smile crept up on her. She chuckled to herself to recall the time when she'd walked in to find him sitting in an armchair in her living room with his pet cockatiel on his head, how she'd said, "Waya, he's going to poop on you!" and sure enough, the bird defecated in his hair at that very instant. Ahyoka also remembered them baking an apple pie together that she was sure wasn't going to turn out because Waya over-kneaded the crust like it was bread dough, but it still tasted delicious after it had baked. Other things from way back in their childhood came to mind, too.

When she tried to banish these softer memories, it was as though she'd broken a knob on the TV in her brain, and she couldn't turn them off. Not even thinking about her son did the trick.

Instead of the old resentment toward her brother at the thought of her son, thoughts she'd never had before about Will pushed their way into her consciousness: *Will made his own choices. No matter what, Waya couldn't make them for him. Yes, he was young, but he knew right from wrong, and he chose wrong. His addictions, his lifestyle, are his choice. How many times have you begged him to choose right and come home, yet he continues to choose wrong? And how many times was Waya actually present to egg Will on when you tried to get him to stop? None.*

For the first time in ten years, Ahyoka felt blinding rage toward her son instead of seeing him as her brother's helpless victim. But then, almost as instantly as it flared up, the anger dissipated as she realized that unforgiveness toward her son would change nothing. It would only keep her imprisoned and alone with her resentments, as she'd already been for too long.

"But I don't want to live with their addictions, Great Spirit! I can't watch them kill themselves!" she cried aloud. "What can I *do*? Nothing! I learned that years ago."

But you did do something. You walled yourself off from them, closed your heart to them.

"I didn't close my heart to my son!" Ahyoka argued.

No, but you did wall yourself off from him so you wouldn't have to look at what you judged to be a wasted life. You've even pretended you didn't have a son so you wouldn't have to tell others what a failure he is. But you believe ***you*** *are the real failure, don't you?*

"PLEASE STOP!" Ahyoka screamed then crumpled into a helpless ball on the carpet and cried until she couldn't cry anymore.

Chapter Five

Decisions

When she awoke the next morning, still curled up on the floor, Ahyoka hadn't yet faced her own demons, but she had decided that she would go to see Waya once. Whether or not he was comatose, she'd tell him she did love him in her heart of hearts, but she couldn't invite him back into her life because she would never allow herself to be hurt by anyone's addictions ever again. Then her conscience would be clear and she could be done with it.

Arising, Ahyoka went into the bathroom to shower. As she was eating her breakfast, her cell phone rang. It was another 209 number. "Yes, Mr. King?" she said as she answered, certain it was him, and it was.

╬

Waya growled as Jay walked in at 9:00 a.m. for the third day in a row. "What are you doing here again? Did I invite you?"

"I thought you might like to know that I got in touch with Ahyoka," Jay answered as he pulled up a chair and sat next to the bed.

Waya's heart skipped a beat at the mention of his sister. "Why did you think I'd like that? Ahyoka doesn't care about me. I screwed that up years ago when I 'took her son away' as she puts it."

"No, Waya, you're wrong. She doesn't *want* to care about you anymore, but deep down, your sister still loves you. I could tell it in her voice. She's very hurt that you did what you did, and the pain she has dealt with over her son's addictions has been crippling, but Ahyoka was aptly named 'she brings happiness'. She will bring that to you, and to herself—if you'll allow it. I've had several conversations with her, and she's decided she wants to come visit you. Are you okay with that?"

"'Several conversations'? Did you have to twist her arm?"

Jay looked directly into Waya's wounded eyes. "What else did you expect? That she would instantly forgive you just because you're seriously injured? You can't possibly understand the severity of the heartache Ahyoka has lived with, the hundreds of nights she's cried herself to sleep for fear that Will is dead…or worse, the way she works two full-time jobs in order to go to bed so exhausted she can't think about it anymore."

Waya returned Jay's look defiantly. "Sounds like she's a workaholic to me. How does that make her any better than me?"

Jay shook his head. "Waya, you have so much to learn. For now, please answer the question: do you want to see your sister, or not?"

"I guess so," Waya admitted with a grudging shrug.

Jay smiled and said, "I'll be back."

"I'm sure you will."

Chapter Six
Preparing the Way

"Your brother came out of the coma a couple of days ago, and he wants to see you," Mr. King informed Ahyoka.

Even though she'd just made the decision to go and see Waya, Ahyoka wasn't prepared for this, and she almost dropped her cell phone. Juggling the device briefly, she righted it, put it back up to her ear and said, "He's awake?"

"Yes. And I would like to see you, also, before you make the trip to California. There are some things we need to discuss."

"I'm not in the habit of inviting total strangers into my home, Mr. King," Ahyoka said, uneasy.

"We aren't total strangers, Ahyoka. I told you before that we were first acquainted when you were a child. But, if it makes you feel better, we can meet in a public place of your choice. I'm here in Ohio right now. Could we possibly meet in an hour?"

"You're *here*?" Ahyoka squeaked. "How did you know I live in Ohio? I never told you that."

"From the area code of your cell phone number, of course."

"But that means nothing anymore! People move across the country and keep their same numbers now."

"So, I took a chance. I looked up the prefix to your number and found your town. I'm sitting in the Harbor Perk Coffeehouse right now. If that suits you, you can join me here, or you can choose someplace else."

As it was Sunday, and she didn't have to work until the next day, plus she was in dire need of caffeine after the night she'd just spent, Ahyoka thought: *What the heck? He's come all the way from California; the least I can do is meet with him.* "Fine, Mr. King. I'll see you there in half an hour."

Freshly showered and feeling marginally better, Ahyoka walked into the coffee shop twenty-five minutes later. She glanced around the long, narrow room, looking for an older gentleman. But there was no one who even remotely fit that description. As she turned around to leave, thinking she'd been hoodwinked, although for what reason she couldn't begin to fathom, a man in his early thirties arose from a round table in the back and called, "Ms. Ridge?"

This can't possibly be the man who knew me as a child! I'm 48 now, and he's way younger than me. Is this some kind of super scam my brother instigated? Ahyoka's hackles rose at the thought.

She stalked toward the table, ready to give this Mr. King a blistering piece of her mind for playing games with her. But as she drew nearer, a strange feeling of déjà vu descended, as well as a calming sense of peace, and the angry words she'd planned to speak were gone, as if she'd never thought them in the first place.

Pulling a chair out, Jay King said, "Have a seat, Ahyoka."

"I'm not sure I should, really. I'm having trouble reconciling the person I see in front of me with the person who knew me as a child. You seem much too young."

"Oh, I assure you, I'm not. Now, would you like to sit down?"

"Actually, I haven't had my breakfast or morning cup of coffee yet. I'm going to place my order then I'll join you."

"No, I'll join you, my treat. I only had a glass of water while I waited for you." Mr. King pushed the chair back in and followed Ahyoka to the counter.

She ordered a big mug of Bula Breakfast Blend and a blueberry muffin. Her companion asked for a small cup of the same and also had a muffin, although he chose chocolate, chocolate chip.

He grinned at her, his radiant smile transforming his rather solemn face, and said, "I have a terrible sweet tooth." Then he paid the cashier, and they returned to the table, which miraculously hadn't been claimed by other customers in their absence.

Once seated, Ahyoka asked, "How is it, Mr. King, that you know my brother?"

"Oh, call me Jay, please. I've known your brother since he was born, although he never knew me until two months and two days ago, when I picked him up off the roadside."

This man seemed to be completely sincere, but looking into his youthful face and tawny brown eyes, Ahyoka was again assailed by disbelief, not only about the length of time he claimed to be acquainted with Waya, but also that her brother could possibly have "known" Jay while he was in the coma.

As if he'd read her thoughts, Jay said, "People are aware of many things while comatose; sometimes they recall things that happened, and sometimes they don't."

"I have heard that," Ahyoka agreed slowly. She'd give Jay the benefit of the doubt on that one.

"I believe your brother is on the verge of 'turning over a new leaf' as the old cliché goes. But he needs your help to do it. Will you fly back with me to California today and go see him? I bought two tickets, one round-trip, and I'll take care of all the accommodations."

Resistance was Ahyoka's first reaction. "Wait a minute! You asked me on the phone to come and see Waya, not to come with *you* to see him. And what's all this about me helping him to turn over a new leaf? I told you already, I'm not his keeper. Plus, why would I go anywhere with someone I don't really know? This just seems like one big con game to me. I'll bet Waya's not even in the hospital, and what's really going on is that he's roped you in to somehow sucker me out of what little savings I have."

Jay shook his head and looked at her with compassion. "No, Ahyoka, it's not a con. I only want to help you."

Ahyoka snorted and jumped up from her chair, coffee half-drunk, muffin half-eaten. "By getting me to 'help' my brother? I don't think so. Goodbye, Mr. King."

"I'll be right here for another hour if you change your mind."

"I doubt it, Mr. King," Ahyoka threw over her shoulder as she headed for the door.

╬

The first thing Ahyoka did when she got home was look up the number for Kindred Hospital using a search engine on her phone. Once connected to the receptionist, she asked, "Is Waya Ridge a patient there?"

"Let me check. One moment, please," the polite female voice replied. There was a brief pause then, "Yes, Waya Ridge is a long-term patient here. He's in Room 133."

"Thank you," Ahyoka said and hung up.

So, Mr. King hadn't lied. The brief respite from the incessant worry she'd felt over her brother while she had believed this all to be a hoax came to a crashing halt and renewed anxiety over Waya took its place.

No matter what she did, she couldn't escape it. She had to do something, or she'd go crazy. She paced the kitchen for a few minutes, then sighed and gave in. "Fine, Mr. King!" she yelled as if he was there with her. "Have it your way!"

Going to her bedroom, she packed a suitcase with enough clothes for a couple of days then locked up and drove back to the coffeehouse.

╬

They flew out of Cleveland at 2:30, and as they sat together in first class—a luxury that Ahyoka had never before been able to experience—the conversation that had never really ended between them resumed.

"So, Ahyoka, do you recall how you once roamed the forests and fields with your brother?" Jay asked as the plane left the runway and began to gain altitude.

The question startled her. How did he know that? Oh, right, Waya must have told him about it.

Ahyoka allowed herself a small smile. "We were such little heathens! Gallivanting all over the place unsupervised, sneaking into people's orchards and picking fruit off the trees, or out of melon patches, or helping ourselves to vegetables in the fields. Waya and my other brothers even 'tickled' some salmon right from a man-made run. We got caught a couple of times but managed to weasel out of trouble by lying about where we lived." She shook her head, feeling a little guilty, but not much, about it now.

"I suppose you managed to survive some very rough times when you would have otherwise gone hungry by doing what you did," Jay remarked. "And in Heaven everything belongs to everyone, anyway, as it should on here on earth."

"Well, that's why it doesn't bother me too much that we did that, actually. I know my Cherokee ancestors believed the same way. They thought stealing horses from other tribes was a silly game, a coup. But it did make me feel guilty the few times I stole some sweets from the store as a kid. Those instances weren't necessary."

"Guilt isn't necessary, either. I gather that Waya stole a whole lot more than a few sweet treats, and I know you judge him for that. Judgement isn't needed, only forgiveness. Forgive him, and you'll find it so much easier to forgive yourself. That's all God wants, for the whole world to forgive and return to Him."

Two stewardesses pushing a cart interrupted them to pass out snacks and ask if they wanted to order something to drink.

"I'd like a Sprite, please," Ahyoka said.

"I'll have the same," Jay added.

Ahyoka, used to having to pay for drinks in economy class, reached for her purse.

Jay put a hand over hers to stop her and whispered, "Drinks, snacks and meals are free in first class, and even if they weren't, *everything* is on me. I already promised you that."

"Thanks," Ahyoka whispered, her cheeks coloring slightly as she popped the top on her can and poured the soda into the cup of ice that had been provided.

Not wanting to feel better toward him, Ahyoka shook off her warm feelings for Waya with grim determination and said, "I have to tell you, Mr. King, that I'm not so sure I *can* forgive Waya. There's an awful lot you don't know about. The fun we sometimes had as kids doesn't change that."

"Please, call me Jay, and if by 'an awful lot' you mean how Waya led your son into drugs and life on the streets, I realize that he's made some grievous mistakes. But, haven't you made some serious mistakes of your own?"

Ahyoka was silent, recalling some of those "serious mistakes", like even getting involved with Will's father in the first place then marrying another man who was just as bad, dragging her son through the mud of a very dirty, disastrous, abusive marriage.

Her worst mistake was not being there for Will since he was a baby due to constantly working. For the millionth time, she castigated herself for that; perhaps if she'd just gone on welfare and been there for Will when he got home from school, given him much more love and attention than he'd gotten from her, he wouldn't have felt the loss of a father as much or been so easily swayed by her brother.

Her brother—actually, *that* was the biggest mistake of all. She should never have let Waya come around as an adult. She knew he was trouble, and she had invited it right in.

"Ahyoka," Jay said, interrupting her thoughts, "I didn't say that to make you feel bad. I know you tried your best with Will, wanting to give him more than the meager existence you would have had on public assistance. Also, you were brainwashed very young concerning substance abuse, and physical abuse, for that matter. Your parents repeatedly told you that you didn't see what you saw, so you were blind to those traits in the men you were attracted to."

How does Jay know this? Waya definitely couldn't have told him about my innermost thoughts and feelings. Ahyoka was so stunned, she couldn't have uttered a word if she wanted to.

Continuing, Jay said, "And as for allowing your brother to come and visit, can't you see that was an extension of the very same thing? You were trained since you were a tiny girl—by parents who were too busy using substances and abusing each other to take care of their children themselves—that it was *your* duty to take care of your brothers. When it came to them, you had emotional blinders on."

Who ***is*** *this man? Does he have ESP? Is he reading my thoughts?* But even as these musings occurred, Ahyoka realized she hadn't ever thought about being brainwashed or having "emotional blinders" on. A shiver ran down her spine, but it was not one of fear. Somehow, she was beginning to believe that Jay King really did have her best interests at heart.

This was proved by what he said next: "You must learn to forgive, Ahyoka—forgive your brother, forgive yourself. There is nothing in this world that forgiveness cannot heal." He reached over and patted the top of her hand as it lay on the armrest between them. "Now, as a means to an end, let's hear some more of those escapades of yours, particularly those involving Waya."

"I have the strangest feeling that you already know all about them," Ahyoka said.

Jay grinned over at her and said, "Maybe, but it will be so much more fun hearing about them from your point of view."

During the next three hours until the plane landed at LAX, the conversation continued to focus on the relationship Ahyoka had had with Waya when they were kids. As Jay prodded memories out of her and she related various anecdotes that came to mind, Ahyoka was amazed at his knowledge of her and Waya. It still seemed surreal that he knew all he did, but Jay made her feel so at ease—laughed and made her laugh as she walked down memory lane with him—that she began to let go of her fears and relax. She didn't begin to understand it, but it seemed this man did know her—and Waya—truly.

Chapter Seven
Reunion

On the morning of the fourth day, Waya felt much better, less disoriented, more alert. It was almost nine, and he had not lost consciousness once so far. He suddenly realized that he also hadn't had a craving for his drugs or heard the voices of his imps taunting him since he'd first awoken from the coma. When Sadie came in to check on him, he asked, "Why aren't I having withdrawals?"

Sadie said, "Because you had them while you were in the coma. That's what the doctor prescribed the morphine for, to ease your apparent discomfort even though you were unconscious. Heroin, right?"

"Yeah," Waya admitted. Privately, he thought it was awesome that he had been spared any awareness of the terrible withdrawals he'd gone through a few times before when he couldn't get his fix. But he still thought it was odd that he hadn't had any kind of craving whatsoever, not even for a cigarette or some beer, and it had been a few days since he had come out of the coma. He wasn't yet aware of how long he'd been in it.

Another thing he thought was strange was that his liar imp hadn't shown up, either. Being untruthful about pretty much everything—even when it wasn't necessary to get him out of trouble—had been a life-long habit of his.

Just then Mr. King arrived, as always at 9:00 AM precisely. Ahyoka—looking pretty much the same as she had the last time he'd seen her about six years ago, except maybe more tired around the eyes—walked in behind him. Jay set his chair next to Waya's bedside, as usual, but his sister hung back, still standing just inside the doorway, looking like she might run out of it again at any second.

"Pull up a chair, Sissy," Waya told her, the old nickname coming easily to his tongue. He nodded toward his overbed table. "You can roll this out of the way and put your chair in its place."

The sight of her brother, so weak, emaciated and street-worn, his stubbly hair growing in around a long, jagged, red scar that ran from just an inch or so above his forehead along the top of his head to the crown, obviously still healing, nearly did Ahyoka in. Unbidden, a rush of emotion hit her, and tears sprang to her eyes, which she hid by turning her back to Waya as she positioned her chair.

By the time Ahyoka sat down, she'd barricaded the wayward feelings of horror and sympathy behind the wall that her conscience had accused her of building. "Hello, Waya. How are you?" she asked in a studied monotone.

His sister's seeming lack of concern rankled. "How do you think I am?" Waya snarled.

Ahyoka jumped up from her chair. "I'm sorry, Mr. King. This was a mistake," she said, heading for the door.

"Ahyoka, please stop. I'm sorry. I was out of line. I'm having a hard time coping right now. I didn't mean to speak to you that way. You don't deserve it. Please stay." Waya spoke a truth that shocked his sister almost as much as seeing him this way had. She had never before known him to own up to anything.

Glancing over her shoulder, she saw that Waya's face had crumpled and he was crying. She pivoted, went back to his bedside, sat down and took his hand, careful not to dislodge his IV. This time, she let the tears that filled her eyes show.

"What is it going to take for you to stop, Waya? Do you *want* to die?" she cried.

"I did," he admitted. "I'm still not sure that I don't, but hey, at least I got clean." He laughed his Muttley, the sneaky cartoon dog, laugh.

Ahyoka had forgotten Waya did that and, caught off-guard, she chuckled.

Jay, who'd been silently observing the dynamics between the siblings, laughed, too.

"Seriously, Sis, I don't know how I feel. I don't even know how long I've been here."

"At least two months," Ahyoka replied.

"Two months and four days, to be exact," Jay added.

"Two months! I gotta get out of here!" Waya tried to lift up so he could yell for one of the staff, but his head flopped right back down the way a baby's does when it's unsupported.

Jay put a gentle but firm hand on his shoulder. "Waya, you should know you're in here for at least another few months. You haven't remained completely coherent or conscious for one whole day yet, and you'll need extensive physical therapy to regain full movement of your limbs. Despite the daily attention of a physical therapist, they've weakened in the time you've been lying in this bed."

"But, I gotta find Will!" he cried. "Will doesn't know what happened. He'll think I just deserted him! He's all alone out there now."

"And whose fault is that?" Ahyoka accused, removing her hand from her brother's, her heart hardening again.

"Ahyoka, does your unforgiveness change anything now?" Jay asked in a mild tone.

The question pulled her up short. "Well, no."

"Perhaps Waya has another reason why he wants to find Will. Do you, Waya?"

But Waya had lost consciousness again.

"Is he okay?" Ahyoka asked, as Sadie came in and checked her patient's monitor and made some notations on his chart.

"Yes, this is typical of someone who's been in a prolonged coma. Mr. Ridge is doing better each day, but he'll keep going in and out for a while yet." Sadie patted Ahyoka's shoulder, smiled over at Jay, and left the room again.

Jay looked intently at Ahyoka and said, "You must forgive, Ahyoka—forgive your brother, forgive yourself. There is nothing in this world that forgiveness cannot heal. I have said this before. It is the only thing God really wants: for all His prodigal sons and daughters to find their way back to Heaven and Him through the power of forgiveness for themselves and others. Next to love, it is the greatest power on earth."

Ahyoka, still warring within herself, looked away.

Waya returned to consciousness again. He seemed disoriented for just a few seconds, then asked Jay, "Can you please help me find Will?"

Before Jay could answer, Ahyoka demanded, "Why, Waya? So you can further ruin him?"

Struck dumb with a remorse he'd never before experienced, Waya couldn't answer, but Jay did.

"Waya, your nephew is safe in God's hands, no matter what his physical circumstances seem to be. You both were 'bums on the street', and while that lifestyle didn't seem to teach *you* anything, perhaps it is a lesson in humility for Will, just as your accident brought you here so you could learn what you are learning. God is always with him, in fact has never left him, but it is up to Will to awaken and forgive, too. Your job is your own forgiveness now that you are finally beginning to awaken."

Ahyoka couldn't contain herself and blurted, "I have begged Will to see the light! I have pleaded time and again with him to change his ways and come home!"

"Ah, dear mother, how could he respond as you wished when your request came out of the shadows, too? When your own heart is still shrouded in such darkness, such fear? Worry not for your son; nor for yourself, but seek the kingdom of Heaven first, and you will see its light truly."

"How do I find 'the kingdom of Heaven'? I've tried reading the Bible and going to church, and all it did was make me feel worse, more confused."

"Forgive, Ahyoka, forgive seventy times seven, and even more than that. Forgiveness is the key that will open Heaven's door. You need do nothing else."

"It's too hard!" She glared at her brother. "Waya, I don't think I can *ever* forgive you for taking my beautiful, healthy son and making him into a carbon copy of you!" Ahyoka broke down and sobbed into her hands.

Jay told Waya, "I apologize for the upset, Waya. I'll take Ahyoka out of here. This visit needs to end, but we will return."

"I know, at nine a.m. tomorrow, right?" Waya grinned crookedly, feeling like wailing himself.

Chapter Eight
Reconciliation

Jay guided the still sobbing Ahyoka out of the hospital to his Camry and helped her into it. Then he just sat there in the driver's seat and waited for several minutes until his passenger calmed herself.

Fumbling in her purse for a small packet of tissues and extracting a couple, Ahyoka blew her nose and dried her tears then said, "I'm sorry, but I can't do this. I thought I could when I was joshing with you about the two of us as kids, but it's different now that I've seen him. It stirs everything up all over again. I feel really bad for Waya, but I feel worse for Will and for myself. I know that it's Will's choice now, but Waya led him the wrong way when he was on the verge of manhood and so very impressionable."

"Don't you think the same thing happened to Waya, Ahyoka? That he was hoodwinked into making all wrong turns when he was young? In fact, Waya was much younger than Will, still a little child, when evil influences began to sway him. Waya loves Will the only way he knows how, and he believed he was being a terrific uncle to his nephew by showing him a good time."

Ahyoka's mouth twisted. "Yeah, he showed Will a 'good time' all right—party 'til you die. That's what I'm afraid will happen to my son, and I'm finding it hard not to hate Waya for it, even now."

She looked out the car window to hide the fresh tears that spilled down her cheeks. "Can you please take me to the airport after I've re-packed my suitcase at the hotel? I'd like to go home now."

Jay sighed, just a little. "You do have a round-trip ticket, and you can change it to suit, but are you sure that's what you really want?"

Sighing herself, Ahyoka said, "No. What I really want is to drive around LA until I find my son and bring him home with me, but I know that would be like looking for the proverbial needle in a haystack. So, yes, it's what I want."

"If you're sure then, of course. Would you please have lunch with me first?"

"You're not going to try to talk me into staying, are you?"

"Scout's honor." Jay held up his right index, middle and ring fingers, thumb crossing his palm to hold his pinky down in the well-known sign for keeping a promise.

"I can't believe you were ever a Boy Scout!" Ahyoka laughed. "You just don't seem like the type."

"I wasn't," Jay grinned. "But I know how to make the sign of the troop and how to keep my word."

"Okay, then. Let's have lunch."

Jay surprised her by stopping at a take-out deli where they could order their lunches to go. "I have a place in mind for a picnic," he told her when she raised her eyebrows in a silent question.

After they ordered sandwiches, chips and sodas, Jay took Ahyoka to the beach below the site of the accident, but she had no idea that was what he'd done. He spread a blanket out on the sand, and they lounged and enjoyed the spectacular view of the Pacific Ocean while they ate.

After they were finished, Jay nodded his head in the direction of the cliffs and said, "Right up there is where it happened."

Ahyoka's dark eyes flashed. "What about Scout's Honor, Jay? You're just trying to make me feel bad by bringing me here so I'll stay, aren't you?"

He replied, "Ahyoka, I said I wouldn't try to convince you to stay, and you do have the choice. I would just like for you to consider this: you can't save your son right now, but you have a brother who can be redeemed. The coma allowed him to get the drugs and the desire to use them completely out of his system. He's so close to choosing the right path. All he needs is a little love, a little forgiveness to set his feet in the right direction. You don't even have to show Waya a LOT of forgiveness, just a tiny kernel, whatever you can 'mustard' up. (That's a little joke, get it? Faith—or in this case forgiveness—like a mustard seed?)"

No smile from Ahyoka was forthcoming. She was still mad at being manipulated, and she'd never had much faith in anything. Life had been too capricious.

Shrugging, Jay said, "Oh, well, I never was a 'Master' at puns." Then he continued, "I believe spending just a week or two longer with an attitude of openness—simply showing up for Waya—will be the catalyst he needs to change once and for all. And didn't you promise him if he ever had a change of heart, you'd be there for him?"

"How do you know that?" Ahyoka asked then shook her head. "Never mind."

"Well?" Jay coaxed with that winsome smile of his.

"All right," Ahyoka muttered. "I did write that in a card I once sent him. I won't promise how long, but I'll at least stay a few more days."

Jay's smile nearly outshone the sun. "You won't regret it. I promise."

"We'll see… I do have to call my supervisors tomorrow and make sure I can get the extra time off."

"With all the hours you've put in, I'm sure you've racked up some vacation time. And if you let them know it's a family emergency, I'm sure they will be very understanding."

How does he know my work habits? But, once again, Ahyoka dismissed the thought. It no longer mattered how this man knew all about her; she trusted him like she had never trusted anyone in her life, and that was the strangest thing of all.

╬

The next morning at nine, they were back at the hospital. Waya's eyebrows rose in surprise when he saw his sister entering the room behind Jay. "I thought you were leaving," he said.

"I was," Ahyoka replied, "but Jay talked me into staying a bit longer. I hope I won't regret it." She shot her brother a meaningful look.

"I don't know why you would; it's not like I can do anything to you, or to Will, lying here in this bed. But, I do want to say I'm sorry, Sissy. I never saw things this clearly before. I never cared to."

Ahyoka's heart swelled with emotion. Waya saying he was sorry was no small thing. Perhaps Jay was right and he *was* ready to turn over a new leaf.

Her throat was so tight she had to swallow hard before she responded. She walked over to his bedside and took his hand. "Waya, I never thought I'd see this day. If you're truly sorry and want to make a new start, without drugs, I'll do whatever I can to help you. I promised you that, remember?"

Waya said, "Well, I don't know if I can change all that much, but I promise to send Will home to you and not mess with him anymore, if and when I can ever find him. I know now how wrong that was."

Pinning him with a piercing stare, Ahyoka said, "You can't possibly be thinking of going back to using and life on the streets!"

"I don't have any desire to start using again, Sis. That's one thing the accident and coma did for me. It got the heroin out of my system for good." He shrugged. "But life on the streets is all I know; it's all I have. I can't get a job anymore. Nobody wants to hire an ex-felon and an ex-druggie, I should know."

Jay cut in. "Waya, don't worry about tomorrow. What you need to do right now is to get yourself wholly well and let the future take care of itself."

"Easy for you to say," he muttered.

Tempted to offer to let him stay at her place once he was well, Ahyoka bit down hard on her lower lip. She couldn't, wouldn't do that. Not unless she was one hundred percent sure Waya was clean forever and wouldn't revert to sponging off her if he couldn't find a regular job.

There were still ways to make money, like doing yardwork or housework for people. She and all her siblings, but she and Waya especially, excelled at cleaning because their father was an ex-marine and insisted on what he called "sparkle clean". Their mother sure wouldn't housekeep; she was too busy partying with her friends.

Waya was also capable of landscaping. Ahyoka had once watched him fell a rotten old oak, and he'd done a beautiful job, cutting it down limb by limb then sectioning the branches and trunk into pieces that would fit neatly into a woodburning stove or fireplace, and he hadn't left a mess behind like a lot of hires would have. He took the time to rake all the woodchips into a pile and shovel them into a bin for use as kindling later.

If necessary, he could even keep her house and yard clean so she wouldn't have to do all that on top of her two jobs.

Realizing she was actually considering the impossible, Ahyoka shook herself and said, "Waya, Jay's right. Worrying about Will or the future is no way to help yourself heal right now."

As she said the words, a flash of insight came to her. She'd been doing the same thing, worrying about the future, especially what might happen to Will. And it hadn't helped at her all, either. Those fears had just kept her locked into habits that were harmful and didn't truly erase them because they were still buried deep in her subconscious, beneath all the overwork. She needed to heal, too.

In thinking she might invite Waya to live with her once he got out of the hospital, Ahyoka realized that, in the past, she'd been playing the martyr—taking care of her siblings after they were grown when they needed to do that for themselves—and resenting them for it. Perhaps she got a certain payoff from it; she definitely felt superior to them.

Then another awareness came, one that was harder to acknowledge. By caretaking others, she didn't have to do the work to take care of herself properly. After her mother died and there were no siblings to tend to, Ahyoka had substituted her two jobs as a means of not looking too closely at what she needed to change. It was a highly uncomfortable realization.

Just then, Jay glanced over at her, his caramel brown eyes soft with compassion.

Did he have the ability to read her mind? It wasn't even a question anymore.

They spent the rest of the morning with Waya. He was still too weak to do much of anything, but Jay suggested a game that he could play—50 Questions. Neither brother nor sister realized that participating would lead to a better understanding of each other, but that's what happened.

Jay offered, "I'll start. Waya and Ahyoka, both of you answer, but not at the same time, and then as we go 'round, the other two not asking the question have to answer."

Waya said, "That sounds like a dumb game."

"No, it's fun. You'll see."

"Okay, shoot." Waya sighed and rolled his eyes as if greatly put upon.

"Ahyoka, you answer first: What was your favorite food as a child?"

"My grandma's strawberry-rhubarb pie," Ahyoka answered without hesitation.

"My favorite was Grandma's homemade yeast bread. You can't buy anything like it," Waya said and licked his lips.

Ahyoka laughed and said, "At least we're in agreement that it's Grandma's cooking! She was the best."

"My favorite food was manna from Heaven," Jay said earnestly.

"What's that?" both siblings asked.

"Well, it falls from the sky like dew each morning in Israel, and you have to gather it before it melts like dew. It's a kind of a seed that, when ground and baked, tastes something like a wafer coated with honey."

"Mmm, that does sound good. Is it anything like baklava?" Ahyoka asked.

"Actually, yes, very like it, except there's no nutty filling."

"My turn! So are you from Israel?" Ahyoka probed, pouncing on the chance to get to know more about this not-so-strange stranger.

"Yes, I am," he replied, "but the town I once lived in isn't on the map anymore. Where are you from?"

"Nope, it's not your turn to ask the question." She glanced over at Waya. "Waya, where are you from?"

"Do you know, Sissy, all Mom ever said was that I was born in West Virginia. And I don't have a copy of my birth certificate. I haven't ever needed one living on the streets, so I don't know what town."

Ahyoka looked thoughtful. "How odd. She never told me where you were born, exactly, either. She said I was born in the town where I live right now, in Ohio. Mom also told me Onacona was born in Allentown, Pennsylvania, and that Wohali was born in the same town as me. I was aware that the two youngest boys were born in California when we lived there after Daddy got that big construction job, but I never paid attention to which towns they might have been born in. I feel bad that I can't even say where we're all from, exactly."

"Well, we were a bunch of gypsies growing up, always on the move. That's what happens when your father is a carpenter," Waya agreed then changed the subject. "My turn to ask: If you had to change your first name, what would you change it to?"

"Why that question, Waya? Do you have to change your first name for some nefarious reason?" Ahyoka said half-jokingly, half-seriously.

"No, I don't have to change my name, Ahyoka," Waya frowned, irritated. "I've just thought about it because some people look down on me more than they already do for being homeless. My name lets them know right off I'm a 'breed'. I've thought I might change it to something like John or Paul."

"Not Ringo?" Jay joked, grinning.

"Very punny," Waya said, grinning back, although his smile wasn't nearly as attractive as Jay's since he only had one tooth left in his mouth, top front.

Seeing it made Ahyoka sad. Waya had once been very handsome, but she still used to hate it when they were young and people told her she and her brother looked alike. Now Waya and Will looked the same, all beaten up and beaten down and old before their time.

Waya saw her reaction to his smile and closed his mouth abruptly. Then he said, "Ahyoka, haven't you ever thought about changing your name?"

"Honestly, yes. Most of you were named after an ancestor, but not me. I've never known why. Since I was firstborn, it would seem logical. I would have liked to have been named after our paternal grandmother, Rose. I've always loved the sweet smell of that flower, and I loved our sweet Grandma."

"Yeah, me too," Waya said softly. "But Mom named us all with tribal names, like hers. At least you got a name that's part of our heritage."

"Well, which is it Waya? Are you proud or ashamed of our Cherokee blood?"

"That's another question; wait your turn," Waya chided. He pivoted his head toward Jay. "What about you? What would you change your name to?"

Jay just shrugged, giving no answer.

"Hey, that's cheating. If we have to answer, so do you. You have to play," Waya insisted.

"I don't have an answer, Waya. I think my name is perfect."

"You think being named after a bird is 'perfect'?" Waya snorted in disbelief.

Jay just smiled mysteriously. Then he said, "My turn to ask the next question. Ahyoka, if the world as you know it was going to end next week, what would you do differently?"

At a loss as to how to answer, Ahyoka said, "I need to think about this one, so I'll have to pass the question to Waya for now."

Jay turned to Waya, "Well?"

"I'm already doing what I'd do differently," Waya said. "No more addictions or lying or cheating or stealing."

Jay nodded and said, "That's true, but what about forgiving and making amends?"

Sudden guilt came crashing over Waya like a tsunami, for he could at last see what he had done, not just to his nephew, to his sister or to himself, but to everyone he had ever robbed, everyone he had ever lied to, everyone he had ever used in any way. "How can I possibly make amends to all the people I've screwed over?" he despaired. "I can't even remember most of them, or I didn't even know who they were in the first place!"

Jay put a hand on Waya's shoulder. "Waya, I don't want you to feel bad. That's not why I asked the question. You didn't see that God lives in you back then—you're barely aware of it now—so you 'missed the mark', or sinned, a lot. That's a hard thing to face up to, but thankfully, God doesn't need you to make amends to 'all those people'. He just needs you to make things right by forgiving yourself for your sins then go and sin no more. That's it."

"That's it? How many people do you know who 'go and sin no more'? I ain't a saint! I can't promise that!"

"I didn't mean it literally, Waya. You're right. No human is without sin. We all make mistakes, and no matter how strong our intentions are to 'never do that again', most of us end up 'doing that' again—whatever 'that' happens to be. But the heart that's right with God seeks to do better and better all the time. That's all He really wants. A willing heart that He can work with."

Waya's eyes filled with tears. He'd been such a crybaby since awakening. "I'm willing," he said.

Ahyoka felt a tightening in her chest and throat. Her brother was ready to change his ways, but what of herself? What would she do differently? The realization hit her that despite all she'd managed to accomplish, she still felt empty and unloved. She had paid too high a price to live in the "real world", had shunned her family, worked too hard to make any close friends, had no one, really. She was all alone. A sob tore from her and she broke down.

After several minutes in which there was total silence from the men while she let everything out, no holds barred, weeping and wailing like someone had died, Sadie came into the room, evidently just hearing the commotion. "What's going on in here?" she demanded, hands on hips, wearing a ferocious scowl.

Jay answered in a soothing tone, "She's just having a pity party that's been long overdue. She'll be all right in a minute or two."

Ahyoka raised a tearstained but indignant face. "Pity party! Thanks a lot, Jay!" She straightened, grabbed a tissue out of the box on Waya's overbed table, blew her nose and wiped her red eyes and her cheeks. Then she glanced at Sadie and said, "I'm so sorry. I didn't mean to cause a disturbance. I promise it won't happen again."

"Hmph. It had better not. Mr. Ridge doesn't need this kind of ruckus when he's just beginning to heal," Sadie scolded and, after checking Waya's monitor to make sure he hadn't been unduly upset, she marched back out of the room.

As soon as she left, Ahyoka glared at Jay. "I thought you were my friend! But you just called what I was feeling a 'pity party'!"

"I am your friend, much more than you know. Weren't you feeling sorry for yourself just now?"

Ahyoka swallowed. "I was, but I have good reason. Waya took my son from me, and now I'm all alone." Back to unforgiveness again, she glared at her brother.

"Oh, so now everything is someone else's fault again? What about your responsibility to provide for your own needs, Ahyoka?" Jay chided before Waya could retort.

Instantly on the defensive, she retorted, "I *have* provided for my own needs! I've worked my tail off at two jobs while my brother and my son just panhandled their way through life!" Ahyoka glowered at Waya again.

"Uh…uh…uh." Jay tutted. "You're still making them responsible for your own lack of communication and socialization. It's not their fault that you didn't find time to make friends, so now you feel completely alone."

Shocked anew—though by now she shouldn't be—at Jay's perceptiveness, all she could do was stare at him open-mouthed.

Gently, Jay continued, "But, Ahyoka, just like I told Waya, you are never alone, and you *are* loved, beloved daughter of God. You just have to let Him in, and He will help you heal your broken heart and begin to reach out to others."

He paused and looked from sister to brother. "I believe the two of you have already begun this process by agreeing to see one another again. And aren't you beginning to feel stirrings of the love you once felt for your brother, despite the pain you continue to blame him for, Ahyoka?"

"Yes," she answered in a subdued voice, knowing that Jay, as always, was right—about everything.

"I'm sorry, Sis," Waya said quietly.

"For what?" Ahyoka asked, sensing it wasn't another apology over Will.

"I'm sorry that you've felt so alone all these years."

Sniffling as a fresh tear escaped her, Ahyoka said, "Well, I've actually been thinking of a cure for that."

"You have?"

"It's not a guarantee; I'd have to be reasonably certain that you're not going to revert to your usual methods of survival…but I've been thinking that you could come stay with me for a while after you get out of here, until you get on your feet and can make it in the world. So you don't have to be homeless anymore."

Now it was Waya's turn to break down. He started to sob, but more quietly than his sister had. "I don't deserve this, Sissy," he said when he regained his composure. "But if you let me come home with you, I'll help you in any way I can. I won't be a lazy bum taking advantage of you this time, I promise."

"If you even tried it, you'd be out on that 'bum' in a hot second," Ahyoka warned, a mock stern look on her face.

Smiling beatifically, Jay said, "There is nothing in this world that forgiveness cannot heal."

"I still feel really bad about Will. Maybe sometime we could bring him back to live with us."

"Waya, Will needs to learn his own lessons, and you'd be enabling him to continue as he is if you tried to do that. Your sister knows this to be true, don't you, Ahyoka?" Jay glanced over at her.

Sadly, Ahyoka nodded in the affirmative. "Waya, he's got to have the same change of heart you've had before we could take him in. But, we *can* go looking for him, see if we can find him, let him know we still love him, and we'll be there for him when he's ready. Not until you're up to it, of course."

"He's a prodigal son who needs to come back to himself and return home of his own accord, just as you two have done. Meanwhile, you can both send the love you have in your hearts to him in prayer," Jay suggested. "Thoughts, especially prayerful ones, do have an effect in this world. That's been scientifically proven."

"You sure know a lot about a lot of things, Mr. King!" Ahyoka teased with a grin, recalling how he'd known about comatose patients hearing things and about the Boy Scouts, not to mention all the insights he had into her soul.

"Yes, well, my job requires it."

"Oh, and what job is that?"

"We aren't playing 50 Questions anymore, so I'll pass on answering. Suffice it to say that I work for Someone very powerful, so I have to know a great many things."

"And when do you have to go back to work?" Ahyoka asked, thinking that she'd have to return to her employment within another day or two, and dreading it. Maybe she'd quit one of her jobs now that she was aware of what she'd been doing to herself by pushing so hard.

"I'm always working," Jay answered.

"So, you're working right now?" Ahyoka quirked a disbelieving brow at the man lazing in the hospital chair.

"In a sense, yes. My job requires me to go where I am needed and help others. My Boss wouldn't have it any other way."

"You've been getting paid to help me?" Waya asked, feeling somehow betrayed.

"No, Waya, I'm not getting paid to help you. I don't 'get paid' specifically for the work I do. But my Boss sees to it that I never want for anything."

"That's how you could afford to fly us out here first class, right?" Ahyoka said. "I'd sure like to have a job like yours!"

"You can, Ahyoka. All you have to do is listen to the still, small voice within you. It will guide you to your heart's desire, if you allow it. It is the voice of God, and God always wants what's best for everyone, including work that is truly satisfying and that contributes to your well-being. It's hard to feel a connection to our Higher Power if we're locked into a hard scrabble life in order to survive. "

That gave Ahyoka pause for thought. When she got home, she'd have to sit a while and listen so that she'd make the best choice for herself concerning work. Right now, it just felt good that she'd made the right choice to give Waya a home.

Chapter Nine

The Road Home

(Two Months Later—November)

Ahyoka was cleaning again, but this time, it wasn't in a frantic effort to keep her demons at bay. Waya would be flying in to Cleveland tomorrow afternoon, and she wanted to have his room ready for him. She stopped in the middle of putting a clean pillowcase on a fluffy feather pillow and smiled.

She seemed to be doing a lot of that lately, especially since she no longer worked the medical transcription job. The book by Oriah that Waya had given her had been the catalyst that tipped the scales to quit. Before she'd read it, Ahyoka had waffled back and forth, afraid to let go, not sure she could make it on the single income from her day job. But because of the book, she'd taken a good look at her finances, figuring in the extra cost to have Waya staying with her, and she saw that they'd be fine. There wouldn't be a lot of extras, but they didn't need them.

Her sleep was sound now, and her dreams were sweet, often of the new man in her life. John had been walking down the sidewalk, and they'd literally bumped into each other when Ahyoka had rounded the corner of the company building on her way to lunch at a nearby bistro.

That was something else that had changed. She now allowed herself to take lunch, to get out for an hour just like everyone else, instead of eating a sandwich hunched over the desk in her cubicle. Before, Ahyoka had rarely seen the light of day. Now that she'd truly "seen the light", she made it a point to eat lunch outside whenever she could. It was this decision that had made it possible to meet John in the first place.

He joined her for lunch at the bistro frequently. He'd been headed into the company to interview for a job the day they'd collided. Now, he worked there, too.

They weren't lovers, but their friendship was deepening every day. John was on a similar spiritual path, and they had a lot of other things in common, too, such as their love of art and music.

Ahyoka had great hopes for a future together. It seemed likely, given the fact that John had just asked if he could take her and her brother to dinner after they got home from the airport. Not exactly a date, but approaching one. She smiled again and hugged herself.

Now she glanced up at the painting she had hung on the wall in Waya's room. Not long after she quit the second job, the urge to create had overtaken her. She hadn't picked up a paintbrush in a very long time, but she remembered the one art class she'd taken years ago and how much she had enjoyed it.

After dithering over whether or not to give in to the nudges she kept getting for nearly a month, Ahyoka finally went to a supply store and bought an easel, palette, brushes, a box with 12 different oil color tubes, and an assortment of canvas panels.

Upon returning home, Ahyoka was stymied. She hadn't a clue what to paint, only the desire to do so. After she set up everything in the little workshop out in her backyard, Ahyoka left it all there to return to the house, feeling like she'd just flunked a test somehow.

Once inside again, she noticed an old photo album lying on the coffee table. Strange, she didn't remember getting it out.

Picking the album up, Ahyoka sat on the couch and turned the pages, smiling at all the photos from bygone days. When she got to the pages with their school pictures, she noticed something she'd never given a thought to before. There were photos of all her brothers at different ages—except Waya. As she continued to thumb through, there was a distinct lack of pictures of him.

Then she recalled discovering—right after one of Waya's visits when Will was little—that a shoebox containing photos she'd been meaning to put into several new albums she'd just bought had disappeared. It had held a lot of pictures of him, so no wonder he wasn't featured!

Her glance fell back to the album as she turned the page to photos of them all in their early to mid-twenties, and there he was, sitting on a stool he'd taken from her kitchen, his foot on the rung with one leg bent, guitar on his lap, long fingers strumming. Waya looked very young, and so, so handsome! His hair was long and a bit shaggy (he hadn't bothered to braid it like he usually did) but the sun streaming into the living room brought out the auburn highlights in it, and he resembled Christopher Reeves, although slimmer and trimmer, not quite the buff *Superman* Reeves had been. Waya's skin was darker, too, which only showed up his dazzling smile all the more.

As she stared at the physical perfection that her brother had once been, at the joy on his face while doing what he so loved—she remembered he'd been singing *Stairway to Heaven* when she took the picture; he'd always liked the songs of the 70's—Ahyoka suddenly knew this would be her first painting. Actually not her first; the ones she'd done in that art class had long since been discarded because they hadn't been good enough in her self-critical eyes. But this would be the first thing she'd paint from her new perspective.

The snapshot was old and had taken on sepia tones, which she'd have to correct using a computer photo shop program, and it needed to be enlarged so she could better capture the details of her brother's face. Still, it would provide her inspiration.

The painting had been finished in less than two days because she'd worked on it almost non-stop the same weekend she'd purchased the supplies. She'd named it *Stair-Waya to Heaven*, which seemed appropriate, given the path her brother was now on.

Two days after it was done, when she got off work, Ahyoka had purchased a little golden nameplate at the same art supply store where she'd bought all the other stuff. She took it to a jeweler's and had the name of the picture engraved on it. Then she went to a frame shop where the clerk inserted the painting into a light oak frame and attached the nameplate to the bottom edge.

"This is really good," he said, holding the portrait at arm's length. "Did you do this?"

"I did," Ahyoka answered, pleased.

"I love your use of light and shadow to bring out the guy's facial features." The young man looked over at Ahyoka, his gaze considering. "Is this your son? He kinda reminds me of you."

Laughing, Ahyoka said, "No, this is my brother when he was young."

"Oh. Interesting title." His lips twitched.

Ahyoka laughed again. "Yeah, it's a play on words I hope my brother will 'get'. It's a gift for him." She thought Waya might laugh, too, when he saw what she had called the painting. She hoped he would like it. She did, and so did the clerk because he said, "Awesome!" and, laying it down, put two thumbs up.

Ahyoka also hoped that the portrait, along with the acoustic guitar she'd bought at a music shop, would encourage Waya to return to his old hobby. Maybe he'd even decide to do something more with it than just mess around, as he had in the past. But whether he pursued a career in the music field or not, just hearing him sing and play again would bring her joy, and she was certain it would make Waya happy, too.

As Ahyoka continued her preparations, she laid the envelope Jay had entrusted her with on the pillow and thought about what she and her brother had both learned from Mr. King over the past couple of months.

Ahyoka had returned home after spending a whole week in California on her initial visit, but she flew back every two weeks—First Class courtesy of Jay—to spend the weekend and monitor Waya's progress.

╬

On her first return visit, what she saw astounded her. Waya was sitting up in a chair, no longer lolling in bed like a helpless baby. He was able—with support on both sides—to hobble to the bathroom and back. Ahyoka also noticed that Waya's hair was coming back in—growing up around the awful scar and making it less obvious—his skin was smoother, less lined, and his complexion less sallow. He was beginning to look more like his youthful self.

Ahyoka couldn't get over his physical progress, but what really amazed her was his emotional and spiritual advancement.

Neither of them had had a "churchy" upbringing. They hadn't read the Bible, and their knowledge of what it contained was limited to culturally accepted practices at Easter and Christmas or what they'd heard other people say. A lot of what they heard turned them off, especially when members of certain religions tried to scare them into converting. Neither of them had any desire to be "Bible thumpers" or "Jesus freaks".

Now Waya talked about God and the Bible like they were old friends. A King James version sat on his overbed table, along with an eclectic stack of books by other spiritual leaders like Deepak Chopra, Eric Butterworth, and Neil Donald Walsh. Ahyoka had never, ever seen her brother—who was a high school dropout—willingly pick up a book in his life!

Seeing the look on his sister's face, Waya grinned and his new teeth became evident. "I know. I never read much before, but now I can't stop. Most people would say I'm a 'New Ager' because I'm reading all this other stuff besides the Bible, but Jay says I'm an open-minded follower of the Christ consciousness, which is found in many, many sources, not just the Bible, although the Bible, especially the New Testament, is still my—our—favorite."

He exchanged a look with Jay, one of student to teacher and teacher to student, full of great fondness and understanding.

Even more startling than these were the changes in his behavior.

A disagreement ensued over his physical therapy. When the therapist, Ryan, a strapping black man in his mid-thirties, interrupted their visit for the fourth time that Saturday, Ahyoka thought Ryan was pushing it, that he would cause Waya injure himself, and in fact, was surprised that her brother hadn't protested. The old Waya would have. He'd have whined and felt sorry for himself, would have said, "I can't do this," and given up.

Ahyoka protested, "Don't you think four sessions of therapy in one day is a bit much?"

Ryan answered, "Oh no, four sessions isn't even the norm. Waya has committed to five a day, except Sundays, so he can get out of here quicker."

Rather than the anger he would have reacted with in the past whenever his sister meddled in his business, Waya displayed calm. He said, "Sis, I'm okay; it's not your job to worry about me anymore, remember?" and the look he gave her as he allowed Ryan to wheel him out of the room was loving and forgiving.

On Ahyoka's second return, Waya was ambulating without assistance, using a walker. He talked at length and with great joy about what he was learning spiritually then said, "Sis, I'd like to give you something to read when you have time, if that wouldn't bother you."

Ahyoka didn't know why, but she felt compelled to seek Jay's direction. When he nodded encouragingly, she said, "Okay, Waya. I'll try to get through it before my next trip."

"I won't start with the Bible, that's a BIG book, and it's written in old English, like Shakespeare. I remembered you said you were having trouble understanding *Romeo and Juliet* when you were in high school, so I asked Jay to pick out a different book for you."

He handed her a slim volume written by a woman named Oriah. "Jay says this one will be good for you to start with. This lady has written a beautiful poem I think you'll like, and she tells it like it is, doesn't sugarcoat what she's been through on her journey. She's been guilty of overdoing it, like you. I've already read it, and I think Jay's right. It might help you slow down and listen to your inner guidance."

Even though Waya hadn't spent his own money on the gift, he *had* spent some real consideration of her in obtaining it, and Ahyoka was touched.

"Thank you, Waya!" she said, hugging him freely for the first time since they were young.

"There's more." He reached into a bag that Ahyoka just noticed sitting on the floor between his bed and table and withdrew a daily planner. "I'm keeping one of these now, and I thought you might like to start doing that, too."

He handed her the planner. She started looking through it, discovering that each month was separated by divider pages on which the month and year were written along with sayings like, "Now's the time", and "Be your best self".

After giving her a minute or so with the planner, Waya continued, "I read something every day, not just the Bible or spiritual books, but also different books about the brain and how it can be retrained, then write down what book and chapter I covered and any thoughts that came to me while reading. It's also my new habit to give thanks for the good things that come my way each day. I write each one down and say, 'thank you' out loud."

"That's really great, Waya." Ahyoka beamed at him.

"Yeah, having an attitude of gratitude has made a huge difference for me. I try to find at least three things that aren't the everyday stuff like enough food and a roof over my head, although I'm really glad to have those now, too. You might like to know I'm going to write down that you visited me today, for instance. Then I finish everything off with a prayer—really just talking to God like He's sitting right here. It's my spiritual agenda. I do it every day before I do anything else."

"Wow, Waya, I can't believe your 180 degree turnaround. I never thought I'd ever see the day, and yet, here it is. Since this practice of yours has helped you so much, I'd be a fool not to try it myself. Thank you, Bubba."

Waya's eyes shimmered with unshed tears. "You just called me 'Bubba'. That's the nickname you gave Onacona when you were just babies together, and then you gave it to Wohali when Onacona died. I thought the nickname died with Wohali. I'm honored that you've passed it on to me now. Thank *you*, Sissy. That means more to me than you'll ever know."

╬

The third visit saw Waya walking without assistance although it was stop and go, like he was an old man. Ahyoka smiled at him as he shuffled down the hospital corridor toward her unaided.

"Look, Sis, no hands!" he yelled, laughing, until Sadie scolded him for being too loud.

"Yay, Waya! Way to go, Bubba!" she hollered back, earning her own chewing out.

Giggling quietly as they headed back to Waya's room, Ahyoka whispered, "You've really made progress. How much longer do you have to be here? Looks like I'm gonna have to hustle to get your room ready in time now."

"Yeah, you might," Waya agreed. "I'm doing much better all around. I still have to pass the psychologist's assessment of my ability to function out in the world, but he's gone on vacation and won't be back for another two weeks. He'll be here right around the time of your next visit. So maybe then we can make plans for my flight back to Ohio?"

"You betcha, Bubba!" Ahyoka said, throwing an arm around his waist as they took the last few steps.

He grinned at her and put his arm around her waist, too. "Remember that dance we made up as kids, the Sidewinder Shuffle? Won't be long now until I can 'move in the groove' again, so you'd better watch out!"

Both of them were smiling hugely as they entered the room to find Jay sitting there in his usual chair.

"Jay!" Waya exclaimed. "Great to see you! I thought maybe you weren't coming today."

"I know, it's later than my usual time, but I had some things to do for the Boss. Still, I wouldn't miss seeing you and your sister for the world. You look much more relaxed than the last time I saw you, Ahyoka."

"That book you gave me did the trick, Mr. King. I didn't want to wind up with chronic fatigue like Oriah, and I sure was headed that way. It felt like I was on the verge of a physical and mental meltdown, so I quit one of my two jobs."

"Are you sure you're going to be able to handle having your brother stay with you financially?" Jay asked, but his expression said he already knew the answer.

"Yes. I sat down and figured out my budget before I gave short notice. There's not a lot of extra leeway, but we'll be okay."

"Hey, would you two quit talking about me like I'm not here? I can do some things to help out in that area, Ahyoka. I might not be able to get a regular job, but if you put in a good word for me with your neighbors, I can clean, cook or do yardwork for them, earn my keep that way. You know I'm good at that stuff. We all had to be."

"I don't really know any of my neighbors," Ahyoka said truthfully.

"What about your co-workers?" Jay suggested. "Maybe Waya could work for some of them."

The idea made Ahyoka a little uncomfortable. What if her brother got tempted, reverted to old habits and stole from them? She hesitated to answer a beat too long.

But instead of flying off the handle at her like he would have once done, Waya just said in a neutral tone, "Sis, I promise you'll never have to regret it. I won't steal from your co-workers. I'm not the jerk I was before the accident. I'll never be that person again."

That made Ahyoka feel small inside. She had to stop living in the past, start living now, and she really had to learn to forgive, not just partway, but all the way, and she said so.

"I'm sorry, Bubba. I have to learn to forget the past and forgive you completely. I'm working on it."

"You don't have to forget the past, just let go of the parts that don't serve you anymore," Jay inserted.

"Focusing on what you're learning now is a great way to do that. What I see it is that you and Waya are both like baby birds who are still in the nest but growing every day. Soon, you'll be ready to fly on your own, spiritually speaking."

Remembering the dead baby bird she'd picked up from her driveway with a paper towel just yesterday, Ahyoka shuddered and said, "I just hope that I don't fall out of the nest before that. I'm too shaky to maintain my balance just yet."

"That's where I come in, Sis. Although I'm still 'shaky' physically, I'm pretty steady now in the spiritual realm. I can help you. How 'bout that? *I* can help *you*!"

"Sounds like a plan to me," Jay said and smiled.

"All right," Ahyoka agreed. "We can start when you get home."

"Home," Waya sighed. "I can't wait."

"Well, I don't think Ahyoka should 'wait' to continue what she's started until her brother gets there," Jay said, reaching behind his back and pulling out another book by Oriah. He handed it to Ahyoka. "Here's the second in the series. Spend some time on it each morning for the next two weeks, and don't forget to count your blessings!"

"Thank you, Mr. King," Ahyoka said, accepting the gift. "I read most of the first book on the flight home and finished it by the end of the work week. I really do like the way Oriah writes, and it's easy to follow her suggestions."

"Always call me Jay, like your brother does. No formality among friends, please."

"Thank you, Jay," Ahyoka said with a little smile. "I forgot you asked me to call you that before." She glanced over at Waya. "I'm also following your suggestion to find at least three things to be grateful for every day, and it's already making a big difference in my life."

"I'm glad, Sis. See, I'm helping you already!"

╬

The day Ahyoka was to arrive for her last visit with Waya—after which he would be getting his psychological assessment then flying out to Ohio to live with her—Jay and Waya were watching a documentary on the homeless in America. The camera panned around a compound in the downtown area of a large city. Homeless people lay on the ground like the litter that surrounded them. One man got up in a daze that wasn't just from sleep. He staggered around, obviously still high on some substance, and stepped all over the other sleepers on his way to the main building that housed the restrooms.

Clicking the remote to turn off the TV, Waya shuddered and said, "I'm sure glad that's not me anymore. I really was on the *Highway to Hell*," he made quote marks with his fingers to indicate he was referring to the song, "wasn't I?"

"It's my way or the *Highway*," Jay joked. Then he added, "No, not really. You can make your own choice."

"I know," Waya said seriously. "Stay on the path I'm on or go back down the road to hell. I don't know this way as well as I did that one, but I like it a whole lot better already."

"Just so you know, there is no hell, except for the one you make for yourself here on earth. There *is* a heaven, though. It's when everyone rejoins the Father in a state of bliss you can't begin to imagine. The farther down the highway to heaven you go, the more joy and peace you'll find along the way, you'll see."

Waya smiled at Jay and said, "Thanks to my Roadside Redeemer, I'm finally headed in the right direction. Before you, I would have died and never known the meaning of joy or peace—or of love. Now, my life is filled with all three. I don't know how I can ever begin to repay you for all you've done, Jay."

"You don't have to repay me, Waya. Just pass it on, pass it on, pass it on. Every chance you get. You know I'll be with you every step of the way, don't you?"

Waya, who had come to deeply believe in this man and his teachings, nodded, his throat too thick with emotion to speak.

After a full minute, he cleared his throat and said, "Is this where we say 'goodbye', and I never see you again?"

"Oh, you'll see me again. But yes, it is time we parted ways, for now. You've become self-sufficient enough that I don't have to watch over you every second, and there are still many others who are lost."

Waya threw his arms around Jay and hugged him tightly. His words were muffled against Jay's shoulder, but Jay heard them. "Thank you for finding me."

"You found yourself, Waya. I just helped."

Ahyoka walked in then and asked, "What's this? Are you leaving, Jay?"

"Yep, duty calls."

It was Ahyoka's turn to throw her arms around him and say, "Thank you for all you've done for my brother, and for me. I'll never forget you."

Jay pulled back and looked into Ahyoka's eyes. "You won't have to, sweet woman. You'll see me again. I promise."

╬

Three days later, after he'd passed his psychological assessment and was released from the hospital, Waya arrived at Cleveland Hopkins International Airport. When he finally got to the baggage claim area, Ahyoka was waiting for him. As well as a set of clothes to wear home, when she'd visited for the last time, she'd brought him a small suitcase so he could pack the few things and the many books he'd collected during his stay at Kindred.

Now, she wheeled it from the conveyor belt over to him. "Got your bag, Bubba. How was your flight?"

"Awesome! I've never flown First Class before."

"I know. I loved it, too. I was pretty spoiled by flying that way four times—eight times if you count return trips. But neither of us had better get too used to it. I can't afford to fly that way on my own, and I know you can't, either."

Waya's face, which had lit up at the sight of his sister waiting for him, dimmed a little. "Yeah, Jay gave us both a lot, didn't he?"

Ahyoka let go of the handle of the suitcase so she could hug her brother. "And the best thing he gave us was each other. Are you ready to go home, Bubba?"

Countenance beaming once more, Waya said, "Sure, Sissy, let's go!"

As they walked to the shuttle that would take them to the lot where Ahyoka had parked, she noticed that Waya's gait was as steady as it had always been. He looked like he'd been working out and had bigger muscles than ever before. With his hair cut about an inch from his scalp on the top, it stood up so that his scar wasn't visible at all, and he was nearly as handsome as he'd been when they were young. He resembled Christopher Reeves even more now than he had in the photo.

An old lady saw them walking together and exclaimed, "If you two aren't brother and sister, I'll eat my hat!" She tapped the flowered brim of the straw hat she wore and smiled. "You look so much alike!"

"You guessed it, Ma'am! This is my brother," Ahyoka said with a proud nod at Waya.

The airport was actually west of Cleveland and inland, so it wasn't until just before they hit I-90 at the end of 1-71 that they got a good view of Lake Erie.

"Been a *long* time since I saw this body of water," Waya exclaimed.

Ahyoka laughed, "Yeah, and I thought, after the last time, you might not *want* to see it again!"

Waya chuckled, too. "Yeah, that was one BIG fish I swam up against. Really scared me."

"I can still see your arms going around like steamboat paddles in the water, and when you got back to shore, your face was as white as a sheet. Ha-ha, serves you right for ignoring the lifeguard! Sturgeon can grow longer than ten feet and weigh up to 300 pounds."

Waya's eyebrows rose. "The bad boy I ran into musta been one of those!"

"The biggest one ever caught weighed 216 pounds. I saw it on a documentary once."

"Well, if I ever do swim in the lake again, I sure won't go past the buoys."

Ahyoka snickered. "I hope you don't mind, but I told Jay about the BIG fish."

With a little smile playing at the corners of his mouth, Waya answered, "I don't mind. Is Lakeshore Park still there?"

"Yes. It's gotten way bigger and more popular than it was when Will was little. Now it covers 54 acres and has a golf course, a fenced in play area for kids, and a waterfowl pond. The concession stand is still there but now there are also five pavilions for picnics. And every Sunday in the summer they hold classic car shows."

"Wow! I'll definitely want to see some of those."

"You'll have to wait until next summer." Ahyoka smiled over at him, feeling certain he would still be there a year from now.

"Speaking of cars, I sure like this one. Is it a hybrid? I noticed it's barely using gas, and it's so quiet. I've never heard a car this quiet."

"Yes, it's a hybrid. It's almost six years old now, but it still gets 48 miles to the gallon on the highway. How does someone who has never owned a car and rides a bicycle know about hybrids?" Ahyoka asked, curious.

"Well, I did watch television at friends' houses and in shelters. I heard about them several years back and thought, *If I ever do get a car and learn to drive, I'd like to get one of those.*"

As she merged off I-71 onto 1-90 East, Ahyoka said, "Maybe we can work out a deal, *if* you can pass a driver's test and get licensed. I was about ready to trade this one in on a new model before it loses too much value, but if you can come up with what Kelly Blue Book says it's worth, I'll wait to get a new one and save this for you until then."

Waya looked like a little kid at Christmas who's just gotten a new bike—except he probably wouldn't ever ride a bike again. "Really? You'd do that for me?"

"As long as you continue walking the path you're on, yes, Bubba. I'd gladly do that for you. Blue Book will probably be about $8,000, and you'll also need a new battery in about four years, if you decide to keep it that long. They cost about $2,000 or $3,000. It won't be cheap, but it will be a good car for you. If you can come up with $4,000, I'll let you make payments."

Waya's face fell. "I don't know how I'll ever be able to do that, Sis."

"Never say never, Bubba. I have a feeling you'll be making some good money before too long, IF you stay on the path."

"Oh, I'll stay on it. I promise. No need to keep reminding me, Sissy." There was just the tiniest tinge of annoyance in his tone.

"Waya, I'm sorry; it's just hard for me to relax and let myself believe in you one hundred percent. And it's not just you. Addictions (mine as a workaholic counts, too) have ruined our whole family. I have a super hard time trusting anyone, even myself—especially myself—because of them."

"I understand, Ahyoka, but think of this: Jay believes in me. You trust him, don't you?"

Ahyoka reached over and patted Waya on the shoulder, keeping her eyes on the road. "Yes, I do. Just give me time. I'm sure I'll trust you, and myself, much better after a while."

About 45 minutes later, she pulled her Toyota Prius into the driveway of a moderate-sized, red brick, ranch style house with a two-car garage and a large landscaped front lawn with a circular brick flowerbed as a centerpiece.

Waya whistled. "Wow, Sis! This is a nice place! A lot better than the cramped little apartment you used to have in that rundown old house," he said as he stepped out of the car and glanced around, only then noticing that the grass was overlong and leaves needed to be raked. "But the yard can use some work."

"Yes, it can. I've kinda been too busy lately to pay it the attention I usually do. You could start on that for me tomorrow. But for the rest of today, let's get you settled in, and then a nice man who works with me wants to take us to dinner."

Eyes widening, Waya smirked and teased, "Ahyoka's got a boyfriend, Ahyoka's got a boyfriend!" just as he used to do back when they were teens and Ahyoka mentioned a boy she liked.

"Waya, John and I are just friends, and I swear, if you say that when he gets here, no dinner for you! We'll go without you."

Unrepentant, Waya grinned. "Just kidding, Sis. I won't tease you once he gets here…much."

Ahyoka smacked her brother on the shoulder as they walked up to the front door.

Waya just laughed.

He was as impressed with the inside of the house as the outside. Ahyoka was anxious to show him his room and get his reaction to what she'd done there, but Waya halted a foot or two inside the foyer and whistled again as he took in the huge front room with a brick fireplace dominating one wall and the big screen TV above it on the mantle.

"You sure have done well for yourself since I last saw you, Ahyoka." He left his suitcase in the foyer and started wandering around the house, taking it all in before he finally allowed her to show him to his room.

As he entered, Waya saw that Ahyoka had done a lot to make it a place he would enjoy for however long he was here. There was half of a king-sized bed, so it was essentially an extra-wide, extra-long twin bed, with a nightstand beside it, a 40-inch TV atop a sturdy antique dresser, a big brown, leather recliner, a small dining table with two chairs, a miniature fridge and even a bookcase in which to keep all of his new books.

"I could live in here if I wanted," Waya remarked upon seeing the separate door that led outside, and he'd already observed that there was a private bathroom just across the hallway.

"I did most of this before Will decided to leave," Ahyoka said without rancor, which surprised her. "I wanted him to have his privacy, hoped he'd stay on after high school long enough to get a good start in life, maybe even go to college."

"I'm sorry, Sis," Waya said with true regret, sighing heavily.

"Enough with the apologies, Waya. Let's just forget our past mistakes and go on from here. Anyway, I did add a few things. Did you see?"

"The bookcase?"

"Yes…" Ahyoka drew the word out, obviously expecting him to notice something else.

Continuing to scan the room, Waya pivoted around and saw the painting. He walked up to it and inspected it closely, impressed by the way his young face was painted half in darkness, half in light, and how that treatment of it actually drew a person's eyes to the bright side. It also symbolized—to him, at least—the way he had come out of the darkness into the light in the past few months. A very talented artist must have painted it. As Waya studied it further, he saw Ahyoka's signature, very tiny, in the lower right-hand corner of the portrait.

"Oh my God, Sis! Did you paint this?"

"Yes, a couple of weeks ago, just for you."

Tears welled in Waya's eyes. It seemed it wasn't just the aftermath of the coma that was causing these bouts of almost feminine sentimentality. His heart was full to overflowing, so when the release valve on the overwhelming feelings got turned, tears were the result.

"It's amazing. Thank you, Sissy." Waya gave his sister a bear hug, like he used to do when they were kids. Only this wasn't a trick employed to squeeze the stuffing out of her. Now, he held her so tight because he loved her so dearly.

When he released Ahyoka, her eyes swam with tears, too. She dabbed at the corners and said, "I'm so glad you like it. Did you see what I named it?"

Waya had been so intent on the painting itself that he hadn't noticed the gold name plate centered on the bottom of the frame. "*Stair-Waya to Heaven,*" he read aloud and laughed, shaking his head.

"There's something else you missed." Ahyoka nodded her head in the direction of the opposite corner.

"You got me a guitar? Oh man, I am so lucky, so blessed to have you as my sister! Thank you! But I haven't played in so long, I'm not sure I still can."

"Oh, I'm sure you can," Ahyoka insisted. "You always could just listen to a song and play it."

Waya picked up the guitar, sat down on the recliner and started strumming. Ahyoka was right. He could feel his gift coursing through him anew, as strong as if no time had passed since he'd last used it. Joyfully, he began to sing, "There's a lady who's sure…"

Ahyoka sat on the arm of the chair next to him and sang along, "…all that glitters is gold…" just like she used to years ago.

As the very long song ended, Waya noticed there was something on his pillow. Putting the guitar down, he arose, picked up the envelope, opened it and took out a sheet of paper. It read:

Waya,

You nicknamed me your "Roadside Redeemer", but I'm also AAA for your soul. Don't hesitate to call whenever you need assistance.

J

He grinned from ear to ear and showed the note to Ahyoka saying, "Well, how 'bout that? I'll bet J knew you'd be offering me your car on the way home. He's got a super sixth sense. You know who 'J' is, don't you?"

"No, not really. Just that he's a really good man and an astonishing mind reader. His insights are incredible."

"Well then, I won't spoil it for you. I'm sure you'll figure it out eventually, especially once you've read the New Testament in the Bible."

╬

21 "Then came Peter to him, and said, Lord, how oft shall my brother sin against me, and I forgive him? till seven times?

22 "Jesus saith unto him, I say not unto thee, Until seven times: but, Until seventy times seven."

Matthew 18:21-22
~*Holy Bible*, KJV~

"And thus will all the vestiges of hell, the secret sins and hidden hates be gone. And all the loveliness which they concealed appear like lawns of Heaven to our sight, to lift us high above the thorny roads we [traveled] on before the Christ appeared."

~*A Course in Miracles*, Manual for Teachers, pg. 11~

Epilogue

(One Year Later)

Waya and Ahyoka continued their spiritual journey, meeting together with John at his home one evening a week to share the things they were discovering through their studies. They also joined a group of "open-minded followers of the Christ consciousness" on Sunday mornings at a place they'd never thought they'd end up in—church.

John encouraged them to come to his house of worship, and they loved it. The church accepted every faith, all were welcome. There, Waya and Ahyoka discovered the delight of true community with others.

Brother and sister met everyone on the block as a result of a party Waya threw shortly after he moved in. When Ahyoka arrived home that late afternoon to find her home and backyard overrun with strangers and Waya turning chicken thighs, burgers and hot dogs on the grill, she was very upset.

Without a word, she turned on her heel and went back inside to assess the contents of her freezer. Sure enough, it was nearly empty. *Oh, this is so like the old Waya!* she thought, gritting her teeth. *Just takes what he wants without asking, no consideration for others! I've made a BIG mistake.*

She stood there holding the freezer door open, hoping the cold air would cool the flames of ire that heated her cheeks, when her brother walked in the back door and came to stand behind her. He put his hands on her shoulders and gently turned her around to face him.

"Why did you do this, Waya?" Ahyoka hissed keeping her voice down so the people wandering around in the house wouldn't hear her. "You didn't even ask, and you've taken all the meat that I bought to last us for the next couple of weeks."

"Sis," Waya said in a soothing tone, "please, don't be mad. I didn't ask you because I was sure you'd say 'no', and I had to figure out a way to meet the neighbors so I can get some jobs. Once I get work, I'll pay back with interest what the meats cost. I asked the neighbors to chip in on all the other stuff: side dishes, desserts, sodas, water, paper plates, plastic forks, knives and spoons, napkins. And they have. They also brought over folding tables and chairs, and when it gets dark we're gonna have a bonfire in the firepit to get rid of that big pile of leaves I raked up. I'll bet you've never even used it yet, have you?"

Beginning to see the wisdom of her brother's reasoning, and admitting to herself that she would have said 'no' to the whole thing, Ahyoka said, "No, I haven't ever used it." She sighed, inwardly also acknowledging that she had failed to get him a job with any of her co-workers—because she didn't know most of them any better than she did her neighbors—and that Waya had come up with a good solution, except that it would strain the food budget for the next couple of weeks.

"Okay, Waya, let's just enjoy the party. We'll probably have to eat leftovers from it for the rest of this week then have stuff like tuna casserole, eggs and fried potatoes the following week to make up for the food you took, but I can see this is probably a good thing."

And it was. Waya did get a bunch of yardwork jobs from the neighbors, and because he brought out his guitar and held a singalong during the bonfire, he was also hired to play and sing at various functions like weddings and birthday parties. Ahyoka benefited, too, by gaining new friends she could turn to for help and companionship.

When he came home from his first job—mowing the yard for Betty, a little, old, widow lady who lived down the street—Waya pulled a twenty dollar bill out of his pocket. "Here, Sissy. First installment on repayment for the meat. I'll make at least nine more."

Accepting the money, Ahyoka said, "It didn't cost quite that much, Waya. Make it four more payments and we're even."

"Okay. Once we're square, would you hold onto my money? I want you to feel better about things, to know you can trust me. Also, I don't have a bank account, and you do. If you put it in your savings, it will earn a little interest. That way, I can get out on my own sooner."

"Oh, Waya, I really am sorry to still have these moments of distrust. I can see you're a changed man. Of course, I'll hold onto your earnings for you. I'll do whatever I can to help you. But you *can* stay here as long as you like, you know. You don't have to be in any big hurry to move out."

"I know. I really like my room, but the day will come when you'll need more privacy." Waya grinned and waggled his eyebrows.

Smacking him lightly on the arm, Ahyoka said, "Oh, you! John and I are just friends."

"Not since he's asked you out on several dates, and you've accepted, you're not. Plus, I saw you kissing him outside the front door after the last date. By the looks of that kiss, you're w-a-a-ay past the 'friends' stage."

Ahyoka blushed and didn't say a word.

Not long after that, when they'd known each other just four months, John proposed.

Eight months later, it was Ahyoka and John's wedding day. They planned a small affair and reception at their church, nothing too fancy because John and Waya, who was slated as best man, disliked suits, and Ahyoka felt that a really expensive white gown at her age was a bit too much. So, she made herself a simple Persian blue dress that hung just above her knees and overlaid it with Venetian lace.

She talked John into wearing a white dress shirt with a vest and bowtie in lieu of a suit. She persuaded him try on some nice vests at a bridal shoppe, and they rented a blue one almost the same shade as her dress.

But she was secretly making him one with a Persian blue silk back and blue and white paisley front panels. She had also found a bowtie to match. That color really offset his electric blue eyes; she'd noticed it before when he'd worn a shirt of the same shade.

In the morning of their special day, after a wedding breakfast of homemade banana nut waffles, real maple syrup, fruit medley, sausages, bacon, coffee and orange juice mixed with Perrier served in champagne flutes (instead of traditional mimosas), Waya started clearing the table. John arose to help him, but Ahyoka waved him back down. "Sit tight for just a minute," she told him and disappeared into the laundry/sewing room.

Vest hidden behind her back, Ahyoka returned. "Here, love, I made this for you to wear today instead of the one we rented from the shoppe," she said as she held it up.

"It's perfect, sweetheart!" John exclaimed, eyes shining as he reached for it.

But it wasn't perfect. Because it was a surprise, Ahyoka didn't have John's measurements and had to guess at the pattern size. The vest hung off John's frame.

"Oh, no!" Ahyoka moaned. "I guess I should have let you in on the secret so I could get the right size pattern. All that hard work for nothing."

"It's okay, honey. I can still wear what we picked out at the bridal shoppe. It's a similar blue, at least." John hugged Ahyoka in an attempt to comfort her.

"Sis," Waya said, "do you mind if I try it on?"

"Go ahead, but it'll probably be too big for you, too."

Waya tried it on, and it fit perfectly.

Ahyoka hadn't realized that his more buff physique would take up the slack because he still looked as slim as John. "Waya, that vest fits as if I made it just for you, so I guess I did. It's yours."

"Wow! I finally get something you made! I remember you made Onacona and the others shirts when you started to sew at sixteen, but because I was in juvie, I didn't get one. This makes up for it. Thanks, Sis!" Waya grinned, did a leprechaun jig in the vest, and they all laughed.

A few hours later, Ahyoka waited in the vestibule of the church, about to walk down the aisle. Waya, in his new vest, stood proudly at John's side as best man.

"Hi, Mom," a voice said from behind her.

Ahyoka whirled around and almost dropped her bouquet of red roses, hybrid white and red chrysanthemums, birds of paradise, and blue anemones—flowers that symbolized love, fidelity, joyfulness and anticipation.

There stood Will, looking a bit old and battered, but clean and dressed in a nice black suit. At his side was Jay, also dressed in a suit, but a white one.

"Will!" Ahyoka cried, flinging her arms around her son and trying not to tear up at the sight of him so her makeup wouldn't run. When she could finally bear to let go, it was Jay's turn for a hug. "Thank you so much for this," she whispered against his ear. "It's the best gift you could ever have given me. We didn't even try to invite you or Will because we didn't know exactly how or where to find either one of you, but we wanted both of you here with all our hearts."

"You're welcome, dear one," Jay told her with an indulgent smile.

As the notes of *Pachelbel in Canon D* began to play, Ahyoka put her arm in her son's. "Walk you mother down the aisle," she commanded.

Jay ducked around them to quickly and quietly find a seat in the back.

"Yes, Mom," Will conceded beaming.

╬

At the reception, Waya proudly performed, singing and playing his guitar. At Ahyoka's request he played Paul Stookey's *The Wedding Song*, for the first dance, and Led Zeppelin's *Stairway to Heaven*, which she danced with Will.

Jack and Diane by John Mellencamp was added to the list of the bride's favorites. This could have posed a bit of a dilemma because Ahyoka not only wanted him to sing it, she also wanted to dance to the song with her brother. But since he had hooked up equipment to play selected songs electronically during his breaks, the problem was solved.

Waya played and sang the song, then they played a CD with Mellencamp's version and danced up a storm to it. Everyone moved aside and applauded the two siblings movin' and groovin' in unison.

"Hey man! You sounded almost as good as the ol' 'Cougar'! And you dance pretty good, too!" Bob Parks, a co-worker of Ahyoka's and John's, told Waya as they left the "dance floor", a space cleared in the center of the community room.

"Thanks, man!" Waya grinned as he returned to the "stage"—a simple wooden platform constructed for the occasion.

When it was time, he took a break and gave his best man speech. "John, you have become a good friend to me—and more than that to my sister," he leered and winked, evoking hoots of laughter from the guests, "over the past year. We have grown close in spirit together, and now we'll bond as brothers through your union with my sis. I love you, man. To John, everyone." He raised his champagne flute of sparkling apple juice. "But, wait, I'm not done yet," he said, holding up a hand after all had toasted the groom. "If it's okay, and even if it's not, as brother of the bride, I want to address the rest of this speech to Ahyoka."

He turned to his sister, "Ahyoka, you were always there for me, even when you couldn't be, and I know that. I was a screwup—not just the screwball I am now." More laughter arose from the crowd as they had gotten to know the wise guy side of the man who mowed their lawns and beautified their landscapes. Waya waited quietly until it subsided; he hadn't intended to be funny because this was serious. "But because you forgave the unforgivable and took me into your home, I have a whole new life today. I am so blessed to have you as my sister. Thank you. To Ahyoka, everyone!"

Ahyoka stood after the toast. "May I have the microphone, Waya?" When he handed it to her, she said, "You may or may not have heard the story that just after you were born, Onacona went into the room where you were lying in your bassinette. Ona was just two and a half at the time. He walked up, peered down at you and said,

'Good mornin' timy baby!' You didn't answer, so he said it again, louder, 'Good mornin' timy baby!' When you still didn't answer he yelled, 'Good mornin' timy baby, TALK TO ME!' You didn't talk then, but ever since you did start talking, you've never shut up."

The attendees chuckled.

Ahyoka went on, "However, this is one time opening your mouth really matters. It means that you have finally grown up, that you've stopped being a 'victim' acting out against the world and started being something much more—a person who's able to forgive and see the many ways in which he's truly blessed."

Ahyoka paused and swallowed. "But you know, you aren't the only one who had that skewed viewpoint of the world. I had it, too. And I may not have acted out, but I sure acted 'in'. I internalized it all, felt victimized and guilty at the same time, so I thought I had to try to fix everything. When I found I couldn't fix anything—not you, not Will, not the people who always seemed to take advantage of me—I tuned out by overworking to the point that I had nothing else; that was my drug of choice."

Sniffling a bit, Ahyoka continued. "If it hadn't been for you, and Mr. King—Jay—I would have worked myself to death and died alone. You, Bubba, have helped me just as much as I've helped you. Maybe even more. You and Jay. And I'm so grateful to have both of you in my life. Thank you." She gave them both a watery smile. "And I'm so glad, Will, that you've come back into my life, as well."

Will stood and held out his hand for the microphone. "My turn." After Ahyoka sat down, he spoke. "Mom, I know now just how much my choices have hurt you. But, I promise you, I'm not the addict on the street I was a year ago. Thanks to Jay, I'm learning the same kinds of things you and Uncle Waya have been learning. I still have a long way to go, but I've entered a faith-based rehabilitation program, and it's working for me."

Ahyoka gasped in joy and covered her mouth with her hands. Will had never voluntarily entered rehab before, only submitted when he had to per court orders, and once he'd spent the usual 29 days required, he went right back to his old habits.

Will smiled at his mother and continued, "Normally, I wouldn't be allowed to leave at this point—I've only been in the program for ten weeks, and you're supposed to be in for at least six months before you can leave for short visits—but Jay pulled some strings to bring me here today. I haven't called because there's also a rule against phone calls until you've been there for three months, and I haven't been there quite that long. But, Mom, I'm going to finish this time, and I'm going to become the person I was meant to be. I'd like to say I'm doing it for you, but I'm doing it for me. Still, I hope this is a good wedding present. I love you, and I always have. I'm only sorry I wasn't able to show you that for so long."

By the end of Will's speech, tears were flowing like waterfalls down Ahyoka's cheeks and she could barely see as she got back up, went to her son, and put her arms around him. She had to force the words around a huge lump in her throat as she replied, "It is a good wedding present—the best. I love you, always have, always will, Will."

At the recognition of the private joke his mom had made of his name since he was little, Will started to cry, too. Mother and son had a hard time making their way back to their seats.

J, who was a guest of honor at the bride and groom's table along with Will and Waya, said, "I didn't call you, Ahyoka, because I wanted this to be a surprise." He was the only one who wasn't sniffling at the table; his smile was one of radiant joy.

Ahyoka smiled back at him through shimmery eyes. "I only need to 'mustard' up a little forgiveness for you, Jay," she told him, making a joke of his very bad pun. "It was a really good surprise."

Most of the guests were also dabbing their eyes, and they would talk about this day for years to come, citing it as one of their all-time greatest wedding memories. As they departed after the reception, they each hugged Ahyoka, her family, and Jay, as if they were members of their own families—and they were.

Prior to the wedding, Waya had made and saved enough money to pay the agreed upon down payment on Ahyoka's car. The money he gave her went toward their honeymoon, since John was contributing his slightly used RAV as a trade-in on a new Prius that they'd both use after they got back. John also had a pickup truck that would come in handy when maintaining their home. He'd moved out of his apartment a couple of days before the wedding, and his truck was now parked in the garage.

Waya got a place of his own while they were away in Paris, a little guest house that some neighbors had available to rent. It was just down the street, half a block away.

After he and Ted, his new landlord, hauled the stuff from his bedroom to Ted's "casita", Waya thanked him profusely.

"No problem, buddy. Just keep up the great job you've been doing on our yard, and we'll take your work off the rent. You should start your own landscaping business."

"You know, I might just do that," he replied, shaking Ted's hand.

After Ted left, alone in his new home, Waya said private thanks to J. "Hey, Buddy. (I kinda liked what Ted just called me, and I know you're my BUDDY, too.) I'm so grateful for all You've done for me, for my new life, and for all the good things that have come into it since I met you on the roadside, even though I don't remember that first meeting. Thank you for all you've done for my sister and my nephew, too. Now I know that You were watching out for the two of us when we were 'bums on the street', that You're watching out for everyone. I'll see you again sometime, I'm sure."

Post honeymoon, Ahyoka allowed herself the sustained joy she found in painting. A new friend she'd made at church—who just happened to be a gallery owner—invited her to hold a show, which was a great success. She still worked at her same day job, but met with John for lunch every day and went home with him at night.

Best of all, both brother and sister had each found a "home" within their own hearts.

~END~

Coming Soon

The Savior in Sunglasses
(Park Bench Stories: Book 3)

He awoke from his stupor to find himself on the beach, his mouth and eyes filled with gritty sand, his face slimy from where he'd lain in a pool of his own vomit—the stench of it gagging him—his head pounding to the rhythm of his heart beating triple time, as though it would burst right out of his chest.

Groaning, he tried to rise but could not. His head fell weakly back onto the sand, this time a few inches away from the puke, thank you, Jesus. Though why he was thanking Jesus for anything, he didn't know. He and Jesus had parted ways long ago.

He wished for the oblivion that had claimed him last night to come back, to take him out of this hell hole, extinguish the fire of this punishing life forever.

Too ill to do anything to stop them, he shut his eyes against the fierce noonday sun while the memories he'd tried to flee from with a fifth of whiskey hounded him anew, flogging him with his utter failure…

Also by the Author

Jesus on a Park Bench
Available on Kindle and in print via Amazon and other online bookstores

(This is a short parable and is suitable for adults and minors. It remained year-round in the top 100 of the Amazon inspirational category for six years.)

Amazon Publication Date: December 24, 2012
Product Description:

A middle-aged woman, alone and broke of the eve of Christmas Eve, finds new hope when she gives hope to a stranger.

Petty Theft
Available on Amazon Kindle and other online bookstores

(This is a short family-friendly mystery and is suitable for minors.)

Amazon Publication Date: July 24, 2012
Product Description:

The heretofore undisturbed gated community of Peaceful Pines is now up in arms over a rash of puzzling petty thefts. Nearly every house has been hit, but not one major ticket item has been taken, even though the thief is so professional the police have dubbed him the Cat

Burglar. He moves so stealthily, no one ever hears him; there are no signs of forced entry; and not a single fingerprint is ever left behind. When the Cat Burglar targets her home while she's there, Cynthia Cambridge finds it downright scary, but that's not ALL she finds...

The Studebaker Wagon
Available on Kindle and in print via Amazon and other online bookstores

(This is a family-friendly historical/inspirational novelette co-written with Pete Campbell.)

Amazon Publication Date: October 5, 2015
Product Description:

This is the story of a young man who sets out on a journey to pick up a new wagon for his family's farm but comes back with a whole lot more than he bargained for.

Co-written by a first-time author and the author of the Amazon inspirational bestseller, ***Jesus on a Park Bench,*** this tale of Rueben's adventures is sure to warm a lot of hearts.

Buried Talents
Available on Kindle and in print via Amazon and other online bookstores

(This inspirational novelette is suitable for adults and young adults.)

Amazon Publication Date: January 11, 2014
Product Description:

Downtrodden Sara Avery once sang like a songbird, but no tune has escaped her lips in years. Taken for granted and verbally abused by her husband and her children alike, the only place Sara finds any solace is in her garden. One day as she hacks at the ground with a hoe like a serial killer with an axe, something flies up and hits her, literally forcing her to see things differently.

As Sara begins digging to uncover the self she's buried deep inside, she's met with resistance from her family. Now Sara has to find a middle ground somewhere in-between doing what's right for her and what's right for them. It will take a Power greater than herself to do it, though. When Sara also rediscovers her relationship with Him, even one of the worst things that could happen turns out to be a miracle in disguise.

Like the Amazon bestselling Inspirational, *Jesus on a Park Bench,* this new story by Shari Broyer with a holiday theme is also great reading for all seasons, not just at Christmas.

Red Skies: The Short Story
Available on Kindle and in print via Amazon and other online bookstores

(This short story is suitable for young adults and adults.)

Amazon Publication Date: December 3, 2014
Product Description:

This is Emmie's story—the story of a young girl who loses her parents in an automobile accident but finds family with her uncle, Jim, only to also lose him a short time later to a heart attack. The skies flame at dawn portending hardships to come, and Emmie, left in the hands of a merciless foster parent who abuses her regularly, has many tribulations. She is convinced that God has abandoned her. But has He?

This "teaser" short is the basis for an upcoming full-length novel of the same name from the author of the Amazon inspirational bestseller, Jesus on a Park Bench.

The Neighbors
Available on Kindle via Amazon and other online bookstores

(This short story is suitable for adults and young adults.)

Amazon Publication Date: March 10, 2013
Product Description:

The neighbors are a constant source of ire for George, whose "Good Christian" halo slips further downward each time he has a run-in with them. His wife, Evelyn, seeks to make peace with the couple next door, but when she also has a "run-in" involving the wife, the chances of that become slim, indeed.

Every Step of the Way
Available on Kindle via Amazon and other online bookstores

(This collection of short stories is suitable for adults and young adults.)

Amazon Publication Date: February 22, 2015
Product Description:

This boxed set, ***Every Step of the Way,*** includes the author's Amazon bestselling inspirational short stories, ***Jesus on a Park Bench*** and ***The Neighbors,*** plus her new "teaser" for an upcoming novel of the same name, ***Red Skies: The Short Story***. Shari is a firm believer that Spirit is with every one of us every step of the way, as these stories all demonstrate.

About the Author

Shari Broyer has been writing since early childhood. Her earliest awards: a 1st place trophy for Creative Writing and certificate for First Runner-Up in Poetry at 8th grade graduation.

Formerly she was:

- Editor in Chief of KSU Ashtabula's literary magazine, *Kaleidoscope*
- Facilitator, Writers' Forum, Barnes and Noble, High Point, NC
- Host of *Writer's Digest* World's Largest Writing Workshop, Barnes and Noble, High Point, NC
- Published in various literary anthologies (most recently her poem "One-Eyed Jack" and "Squirrel" photo were featured in *Wild Edges—Manzanita, Poetry and Prose of the Mother Lode and Sierra*, released August 2010)
- Top 100 winner, *Writer's Digest* 2000 competition—Inspirational category, *Shades of Gray*
- Winner of author Terri Weeding's Little Ole Humor Contest

- Board Member/Editor of *The Desert Rose Newsletter* for the Phoenix Desert Rose Chapter of Romance Writers of America
- Facilitator of Writers, Ink. of Greater Phoenix at Changing Hands Bookstore in Tempe, AZ

Currently, she resides in tiny Ajo, AZ, a town just north of the Mexican border. Shari loves it. Although Ajo is very small; it's also very "artsy" with a plethora of happenings: art shows, music concerts and other events—often held at the famed Curley School, remodeled to house artists and artisans. There's never a dull moment, even in summer, when the town shrinks to a third of its winter population.

If you need a good manuscript editor for hire; Shari will be happy to assist you with editing and also with becoming self-published, should you so desire. She welcomes your feedback at **shariannegaylee@gmail.com**, and invites you to visit her website, **http://sharibroyerbooks.weebly.com**.

Made in the USA
Columbia, SC
14 September 2020

19676469R00078